Praise for Naomi Booth

Animals at Night

'Naomi Booth is a master of the short story, and this collection is stunning.' – **Lucie McKnight Hardy**

Exit Management

'Compelling, formally innovative and beautifully conceived.' – *The Guardian*

'A bittersweet and truthful portrait of people still finding their places in the world.' – *i News*

'[A] compelling contemporary read crammed with insight and compassion.' – **Val McDermid**

Sealed

'Gripping... enough to make your skin tingle.' – *New York Times*

'Marvellous.' – *The Guardian*

'[A] brilliant dystopian distillation of just about all the ecological fears a young parent can suffer from.' – *The White Review*

The Lost Art of Sinking

'A short, absorbing read about losing yourself that packs a compelling punch.' – *Grazia*

'Naomi Booth is a name to watch.' – *Prospect*

Also by Naomi Booth

Animals at Night
Exit Management
Sealed

The Lost
Art of Sinking

dead ink

First published by Penned in the Margins in 2015.
This edition published in Great Britain in 2022 by Dead Ink,
an imprint of Cinder House Publishing Limited.

Print ISBN 978-1-911585-92-3
Ebook ISBN 978-1-911585-93-0

Proofreading by Dan Coxon / dancoxon.com
Cover design by Luke Bird / lukebird.co.uk
Cover image by Mishal Ibrahiom / Unsplash
Typeset by Laura Jones / lauraflojo.com

Printed and bound in Great Britain by Clays Ltd, Elcograf S.p.A.

MIX
Paper from
responsible sources
FSC® C018072

www.deadinkbooks.com

The Lost Art of Sinking

Naomi Booth

dead ink

For Michael Fake

One

I suppose you could call it a talent. A gift, perhaps. Except that I had to work at it. It didn't come straight away. The first time I tried it, I was thirteen years old. I'd cut my teeth on mother-grief, so I wanted it more than any of the other girls.

We all filed into the hall together, the girls of 2B, in our burgundy skirts and uncooperative cardigans, pumps scuffing against the parquet, and the secret crackled silently along the line of us. As we moved into place, we flickered our eyes towards one another, already experiencing a slight shortness of breath: the effect of anticipation. Once the whole school was assembled, Mr Ward began his mono-logue:

Today's thought comes from Jalal ad-Din Muhammad Rumi. Ward's voice rose and fell away with a mystic's cadence. The great Persian poet and theologian. This is what he says to us: 'Yesterday I was clever, so I wanted to change the world. Today I am wise, so I am changing myself.'

As Mr Ward expounded the history of the Sultanate of Rum and the Seljuq dynasty, we girls of 2B scrutinised one another. We checked that no one was starting before time. We all made a show of breathing as normally as possible— shoulders back, chests forward—and some of us furrowed our brows in a way that suggested a zero-tolerance approach to cheating. Then the organ started up. The pages of hymn books rustled towards *Blessed Assurance*.

It was time: the game was afoot.

Whilst seeming to sing, we began to make our breath as quick and shallow as possible. I imagine that we might have looked like tiny dogs, our heads bobbing as we panted between each word. We produced a soft shushing sound then, whipped up by the collective hyperventilation. We kept this up until the last verse, at which point each of us held our breath for as long as possible. The boys around us knew that something was up, but they didn't know what. Some of them started coughing to draw attention to us. Miss Briscoe was standing at the side, anxiously surveying the line of us. Three of us had gone down in the previous week. She couldn't understand it. She'd given us all a long talk on the importance of a substantial breakfast.

But Stacey Murgatroyd had gotten to us first. At a sleep-over the weekend before, she had introduced us girls of 2B to the Fainting Game.

My cousin taught me it. She's sixteen and she's shagging a *policeman*, Stacey had told us. She says it makes you go totally rushy.

Oh, yeah, I've heard of it. The *Dying Game*, Chantelle said. I heard some girl in Barnsley *killed* herself doing it.

Right, yeah, I've heard of it too, Leanne said. Isn't it called Indian Headrush? You can *totally* die from it.

We had all agreed. We would secretly play the Fainting Game every day in assembly the following week. The winner would be the girl who passed out the highest number of times. Or, in the case of a tie, whoever passed out in the most dramatic way. Or, if anyone died, they scored an automatic win. No starving, no faking: it had to be real.

As the hymn reached the final verse I gulped in everything I could. We were a week into the game, and I stood in line, my eyes beginning to glaze with the effort. I didn't know what I was doing, back then. I had dragged the air through my mouth in desperate rushes and it had grazed the back of my throat. I scanned along the line now, searching for the girls who might be teetering. Leanne, at my right-hand side, looked perfectly serene: eyes closed, mouth flatly sealed. She hadn't gone down yet either. Chantelle was looking likely: her cheeks were flushed and her right hand had begun to flutter. I closed my eyes for extra disorientation. I tried to force my weight forwards, into the balls of my feet. I let my head fall back slightly. And then I think it *almost* happened. The darkness behind my eyes began to swim into a kind of phosphorescence. I tried to sink into it, to let my brain soften. But I was still a novice. My thoughts refused to blur. I could feel my brain ticking with concentration, all nerves and electricity; I could still follow the words of the hymnal; I could call to mind my lessons for that morning. And then I heard a scuffle down the line to my left. I opened my eyes and let go of my breath. A clearing had formed around Chantelle, who was curled on her side now on the hall floor. Second time this week. She had fallen, audaciously, into the lead.

I went back to Leanne's house after school that day. Leanne's family lived in a blackened vicarage in the bottom of the valley. Elderly people lived on the upper two floors and were looked after by Leanne's mother. I suppose it was a small private care-home, but it seemed like a far more mysterious and macabre setup back then. As we sat in Leanne's bedroom, the calls of an old woman sirened in, again and again, even when we turned the music up. Sometimes the woman screamed for a full ten seconds.

From Leanne's bedroom window, I could see the old headstones in the churchyard, haphazard and lichen-laced. I rested my head against the glass as Leanne practised her dance moves.

What's wrong with you? Leanne shouted at me, jerking her way through her finale bogle. Leanne loved to sing along to ragga tracks in a dodgy attempt at patois. She came to a breathless stop on the bed.

Is it your mum, Esther? she asked, lying down beside me, taking my hand and stroking it.

Are you thinking of your mum? she asked again, with the salacious solicitude all the girls had adopted since my mother had died. Suddenly, everyone had wanted to be my best friend, to lead me into the girls' loos to share claustrophobic confidences about my grief.

I'm thinking about the game, that's all, I said. I withdrew my hand from her. I just want to know what it's like.

Chantelle had spent a long time at break filling us non-fainters in on what we were missing.

It's fucking mad, she said. *A total trip.*

She saw things, she said, before she went down. *Glowing lights and weird shapes. Like ghosts, or something.*

Stacey had laughed and said she was tapped.

But I thought it sounded like the most sublime thing.

This valley has always been known for inspiring weird visions. We'd learned about Ted Hughes from our English teachers, and how dark Crow had first visited him here in

4

the valley. How Hughes saw Crow creating mankind out of the bog and heather and desolate moortops that surround us here. The landscape that inspired *Wuthering Heights* is not so very far from us. People come from around the world to visit it. You can walk from Sylvia Plath's grave at Heptonstall all the way to the Bronte parsonage at Haworth. You can follow the corpse roads, the old paths across the moortops that people used to walk with coffins. Plath wrote about what she saw here, about *blurs of fog* and *sheepfoot-flattened grasses*. Emily Bronte saw moths fluttering amongst harebells and felt the *soft wind breathing* over the slumbering moortop dead. And as well as this, we all knew about the UFO sightings in Todmorden—that they were seen here more often than anywhere else. There was a famous case: in the 1980s a policeman here found a naked dead body on a coal pile, pristine, as though dropped from above. Later he saw strange, glowing shapes in the sky. Cattle are mutilated in this valley and people often claim to see lights hovering at the horizon. The older kids at school had told us about the magic mushrooms that they harvested on the valley sides—the Liberty Caps, which are soft and tan, but bruise blue when you pick them; the super strong Fly Agaric, red and white like fairytale toadstools, but totally deadly if you pick the wrong variety—and the wild things that they saw together in the woodlands.

When would I get to see something? When would I get to be transported?

I just want to feel something... *different*, I said to Leanne.

Leanne thought for a moment.

You *really* want to get out of your head? she asked. Off your face?

Yeah. If that's what it is, I said.

You know, there are other ways to do it, Leanne replied.

I think I half-knew I was being duped. But I was willing to try almost anything back then. Leanne said she had some *arrangements* to make. She disappeared for a couple of minutes, and then she came back for me. I followed her down to the vicarage cellar, where enormous washing machines sat on top of one another and there were two industrial-sized dryers, to manage the old people's laundry. Greyish flannel bedding was hung out at one end of the room and there was an old stone wash-sink in the middle, without any taps. We were below ground level here, and one oblong window showed us the level of the churchyard grass above our heads. I remember the subterranean cold, and how it seemed to seep inwards and upwards through the walls and floor down here.

My mother was buried in the graveyard that surrounded us, at this sort of depth, I supposed.

Let's get on with it, I said.

So, Leanne said, here it is. The *stuff*.

There were two thick lines of white powder poured out in parallel on the stone sink. They made me think of quicklime.

So what do we do? I said.

I've seen my brother Aaron do it, Leanne said. What we do is, we get down like this.

Leanne bent over the surface, so that her nose was hovering over the powder crystals. She nipped one nostril closed, and mimed hoovering down the line.

And then you suck it up like that. You first! Leanne stepped back, the magnanimous host.

Okay, I said. Alright.

The Lost Art of Sinking

I bent down to get close to the powder. I shut down one side of my nose and sniffed up as hard as I could.

I could feel the powder filling up my nostril cavity, almost like a liquid.

And then I could feel a sharp sting, burning through my sinuses.

Ow, I said. Fucking hell... Ow.

Does it not feel... good? Leanne asked.

It feels... like it's burning my sinuses out, I said.

I was fanning my hands at either side of my nose.

Is it supposed to feel like this? I asked.

Leanne watched me carefully.

To be honest, Ettie, she said, I thought I'd try you on soap powder first. To see if you could handle it. It's all chemicals, right?

She swept her own fat line of Daz towards the plughole.

I think I'll give it a miss, she said.

Oh god, I said. I can feel it at the back of my throat. It's disgusting.

So, maybe we need to, maybe, wash it out? she said.

We ran up to the bathroom. Leanne held my hair while I splashed water into my nose and mouth. I gargled again and again, spitting out something grey and gritty. My tongue kept on lathering.

Later that evening, Leanne's mum said I should be getting home. She said my dad would be worrying. So I wound my way back along the canal path towards our house. My dad would not be worrying. My dad would still be at work. The house would be empty. I slowed down, dawdling in the cold. I leaned against the canal wall. It's enormous, that wall—it seemed to hold back the banked-up earth of the whole valley, which loomed above it. I looked into the water. There were ripples at the edge of the canal where a coot was bedding down. I stared up to the horizon. Wisp of a moon in the watery sky. Dusk over the hills, the last line of light illuminating the moortops. A dog was crying somewhere. Sound travels strangely in the valley: the animal could have been close by, or miles away on the moortops.

If I stayed out much longer, the canal path would be pitch dark and I'd have to feel my way home along the wall.

I suppose it was a sort of intuition. As the last of the light sank below the horizon, I locked my breath inside my body. Then I released it and gasped and locked it in and gasped and locked it in again and again. The air shuddered into my lungs. My throat was raw from the washing powder and the air stung as it moved inside me.

Tiny flittering lights began to appear—in the sky or behind my eyelids, I couldn't tell. My legs began to shiver; the ground beneath me began to shiver.

I stumbled back, into the dark, and hit the wall.

I was only out for a moment, but it was a start.

Two

I grew up in a house at the edge of the Todmorden canal. It was a squat lock-keeper's cottage, blasted back to the colour of sand, and it had fancy gates, which my father had painted gold. Despite his gaudy touches the house was always dark, shadowed by the steep valley behind it.

The day I discovered my mother, it was late autumn. Blue skies and bitter cold. I had walked home from school along the canal path, which was dappled with dead leaves and goose-shit.

Mum had withdrawn from the house almost entirely by then, keeping to her room. She needed rest and quiet, she said. Because of *the illness*.

In her last few months, I only saw her in brief snatches after school, when I was summoned to her studio.

Esther, she'd call out, *is that you?*

Yes, Moira, I'm home, I'd reply.

I'd called my mother by her first name for as long as I could remember, at her request, but I called her *Mum* secretly in my head.

Esther, come up and talk with me, she'd say.

Mum had never been much of a story-teller. But that autumn, she told me tales of her life, narrating them with

9

full theatrical flourish, and I had a glimpse of what she must have been like on stage.

Mum's room was a narrow oblong: two bedrooms had been repurposed when my parents bought the house in order to make a small dance studio. The room had large windows along one side, looking out over the canal, and the opposite wall was mirrored. The mirrored wall reflected the canal, spilling its green, dank light through the space. I used to think that my mother was like a beautiful golden fish, trapped inside a tank that was never cleaned.

My mother often reclined on a chaise lounge, winding herself in cashmere blankets. Next to the chaise was a small, black, lacquered cabinet, which held Mum's curiosities: an assortment of fancy glasses—frosted lilac martini glasses, curlicue champagne glasses, etched sherry glasses, crystal tumblers, a tiny cube of glass with a battered silver lid—alongside bottles of spirits. There were white rings on the top of the cabinet, where residual vodka had scoured the lacquer off its surface, and this used to make me think of *the illness*, and of Mum's liver, blanched and retracting. She often had a small plate of garnishes that she used to offer to me when she summoned me up, as though she had baked me a cake. For the last few months of her life, Mum ate only olives, glacé cherries and curled orange rind, as far as I could tell.

Sometimes she was on brilliant form. She would usher me in and immediately set off on a story, as though she was restarting a conversation from just a moment before. She told me her history as though she was recounting it to a journalist, balancing facts with appealing, atmospheric detail. Moira had, for a fleeting period in the late 1970s, been a promising ballerina. This was when she met Vincent, my father, after her first starring performance. He was, by this point, her oldest, most devoted, and only remaining fan. But when they first met, she had been surrounded by attention and interest. During her one run as Odette, her performance had been received with great excitement, she told me. People had wanted to take her for cocktails, had interviewed her and taken her photograph in the rehearsal room. But Moira's problems had also begun. The pain in her knees was worsening. She had danced through it, and during the later performances the pain had reached a pitch of exquisite intensity, shooting through her kneecaps. She had iced her joints in the early hours of each morning, before bed. And Moira had prided herself on being able to keep going, dancing through it all; her dying finale had become more and more authentically agonised, she told me. Ha!

One night, after the show, she found she could barely walk. The stairs to her flat had become almost impossible. The academy provided several different kinds of 'conservative' treatment first; they manipulated, palpitated and injected her kneecaps. But these interferences all failed in turn, and they decided on surgical correction. Through the long months of incapacity in her pale-green bedsit in Islington, Vincent Freestone made himself indispensable. After reviewing her first performance, he had asked if he might visit her. She was delighted to discover that alongside being a journalist he was an expert on classical music, and a real friendship was born. He was an odd young man, she told me, there was no denying that: diffident, always dressed in an ill-fitting knitted tank-top and a flat cap. There was a gruffness in his manner towards other people which bordered on the rude; but this made his tender attentions to her come to seem more dependable than the easy, effusive sympathy of her dance friends. And he brought her the most surprising and wonderful gifts: black-cherry yoghurts, orchids, instant coffee, chocolates filled with liqueur. He made her whiskey sours and always brought new classical recordings for them to listen to together. After the privations of dance school, spending time with him felt like being at a midnight feast.

When the third operation failed to restore Moira's right knee, my father proposed. He had been offered a good job at a newspaper back up in Yorkshire; he would be able to take care of her. They could afford to buy a house in a Pennine town that was big enough to house a studio, and Moira could teach dance. And she'd be closer to her people, he'd said, who were mostly in the north-west. Moira had thanked him and told him she would think it over.

I was very beautiful, she told me. *It's not vain to say that, Esther. It's just a fact.*

But, she also told me, beauty doesn't get you where you think it might. She had been told she danced too prettily by the teachers at dance school who looked down their noses at her.

No one knew quite what to make of me when I was starting out, she said. *A girl down from Bolton, who danced like a swan and spoke like a duck. Ha!*

When her injury prevented her from dancing, she learned that she had the kind of appeal to men that was in fact heightened by indisposition. During her year of invalidism, she had received three other proposals. *Oh, these others*, she said to me, *these men who proposed before your father. They liked to come and visit me and tell me how beautiful I was when*

I couldn't escape easily down the stairs. They didn't like me to speak.

She dismissed these suitors out of hand. But she considered my father's proposal seriously.

He didn't even compliment me! she said. *But he was always there. He treated me as an artist. We'd talk about music, and performances. I thought that he understood... what I was capable of. As a performer. As an artist.*

She accepted his proposal. She moved with Vincent to Todmorden. She became pregnant with me and retreated into her gorgeous gloom. And then *the illness* set in.

My mother was not suited to teaching. She had tried to teach me to dance when I was very young. But she told me that she could try as hard as she liked and I would only ever be mediocre, so what was the point? I had no natural grace. There's only so much that can be taught. She tired similarly quickly of teaching other leaden girls to dance.

I'm making her sound cruel, but she wasn't. Not deliberately at least. She was pragmatic. She was straight-talking and she often treated me with the distant fondness of an old friend.

In those last few months, we had our best times together. Sometimes, when I arrived home after school, Mum would play records and sweep about the room, blankets clutched to her, talking through the dances and reminiscing.

The afternoon before I found her, our penultimate afternoon together, she put on Prokofiev's *Romeo and Juliet*, turning it all the way up until I could feel the vibrations of the music inside me.

Listen to it, Ettie, she told me. Listen to it with your whole body.

13

I listened. The music begins with the rising panic of the flutes. The rest of the orchestra follows, tension building as the noise increases until—crash!—everything collides and spills over. The sound starts to die away, cascading downwards. The lingering harp, the weird violin screech. The music is like moving water then, pooling, then starting once again to swell.

At this point in the music, Mum dropped her blanket dramatically to the floor. She rose up on to her feet, and they began to flutter beneath her.

You see, she shouted, she's falling in love! The bourrée is like the fluttering of Juliet's heart.

Mum fluttered a while longer. And then she held the bar that ran along her mirrored wall, and slowly lowered herself backwards.

This is being moved, she cried, her voice constricted as she arched her spine, her long white neck bared and the crown of her head descending towards the floor.

I'm swooning, she cried out in that horrible strangled voice again. And it must be spectacular! I stay like this until I'm so dizzy I am *almost* gone. And then Romeo will swoop to catch me.

She dragged herself upright again then in a way that was ugly with effort. She was breathless. She stumbled back onto her chaise. Then she fixed her gaze on the still green water reflected inside her wall.

When Margot Fonteyn played Juliet, she said, in the balcony scene she managed *eighteen* swoons in six minutes. It got even more desperate in the bedroom: *thirty-two* swoons. Romeo has to clutch her by the waist, to keep her from falling, doomed, to the floor. *Sleeping Beauty. The Dying*

Swan. None of these are possible without the backbend. And then there is *Giselle!*

Mum began to sweep her hands around, and I feared she might try to get up and dance again.

I fall in love with a duke, she says to me—or to an imagined audience, because she's looking right past me, so deeply that it takes all my strength. I am so fragile. I flutter on the breeze. I hear of his marriage to another and I am driven mad. I sink and swoon in my doomed adagios. And I die. But still I dance! I rise up from my grave, with the other jilted harpies, to wreak revenge upon their faithless men. But I will have no revenge. I will dance again with my duke and forgive him. Then I swoon back into the forest, back to my grave.

She lets her arms drop.

She turns to the drinks cabinet beside her and pours out a thin, golden spirit.

There is no falling in love without the swoon, she says. The backbend, the sink and the lift in his arms. *This* is the key to classical ballet. This is what the surge of the music dictates. Our oldest romance, *La Sylphide*, ends with a devastating swoon.

She was moving her hands around again, looking more and more distracted.

My earthly lover binds me in a scarf. I let him wind it all around me, trembling at its touch. And my sylvan wings fall to the ground. He has killed me, you see, without knowing what he has done, and I have just let him.

She dropped her arms suddenly and let her head fall back.

And then I am carried away by my fairy sisters, she said.

She opened her eyes again, slowly circled her head back up.

15

Do you understand? she asked me.

I nodded, dumbly, not understanding.

She sighed then and lay her arms extravagantly above her head, sinking into the chaise.

Her eyes were closed. This was the sign that I was dismissed.

Three

Long after Stacey and Leanne and all of the others had forgotten about the fainting game, I was just getting into my stride. I practised in the evenings. The house was empty of Mum by then, and Dad had locked up her studio. I had taken a cashmere blanket of hers, which I hid under my pillow. Some evenings, I would begin with that fabric, caressing it, feeling its softness against my cheek. Then I would lie back on my bed and close my eyes. I would listen to the empty house, ticking around me. I had become adept at knowing just the point to stop if I wanted a headrush; and how to go completely under. It's all about the rhythm of the breath. I would inhale and exhale as rapidly as I could. I would do this in successive cycles, until all I could hear and feel was my own loud raggedy breath. In and out and in and out. Rasping. Gasping. Then I would gulp in one enormous breath. I would seal my mouth shut. Silence then. And pitch black. You're trapped inside a black lung. A collapsing star. A dense, dying interior. You're trapped at the bottom of the sea: beneath the weight of ocean, deep in the abyssal zone. But then: awful animal gargle from my throat. Broken sounds of breath returning. Water spluttered back out of the lungs. Life forcing its way back through.

And then I'd start all over again.

The girls at school had begun to fall in love, though they'd never have spoken of it so grandly. *I like him*, they'd say, sobbing in the toilet, *I just really like him, you know? I think I've... fallen for him?* That's how people talk about it, isn't it? Falling, falling hard, falling apart. I hurled myself at it then too. I wanted to feel that same vertigo. The summer I turned fifteen, Aaron, Leanne's older brother, started giving me lifts in his car. He'd hang around the school gates waiting for me, and Stacey and the others wore even more make-up and lurid bras that showed through their thin white shirts in hot pink, neon yellow, leopard print. Aaron was nineteen, a painter/decorator by day and a boxer by night. He spat a lot and had scars on his hands. He had dark skin and the lightest green eyes. He looked at the other girls in their tiny skirts as though they were the most boring sight imaginable, occasionally delivering them an ostentatious yawn. But whenever he spotted me through the railings he half-smiled, and I clocked it. Then he would kick the ground to make the smile go away, and walk mock-nonchalant towards the car, slightly ahead of me. He sometimes had a bag of chips waiting for me, making the front seat warm and salty-damp when I sat on it in my school skirt.

Some evenings he would drive us up onto the moor tops. The further up the valley sides you go, the weirder the place names become. We drove through Little Egypt, past the row of cottages called the Walls of Jericho. We drove along Pudding Lane and wandered round the Red Water in the gloaming. We drove up Dog House and stopped off at Scald End. One night we drove up Sour Hall Lane, over the cattle grids, along the unmade tracks, all the way to Flower Scar, the old Roman road that tracks up to the very top of the Pennines. We were sitting right at the peak of the valley then, eating our chips wi' bits and drinking pop the colour of anti-freeze. We never said much to one another. In one direction, you could see all the way down the valley to Pendle, the hills beginning to turn blue in the dusk. In the other direction, the valley split in two, forking away towards Hebden Bridge and Rochdale. Studley Pike, blackened and phallic, rose out of the tops down that way.

Aaron swigged on his can.

Little lights began to glimmer out there, like tiny stars caught in the valley sides.

Esther, he said. Aaron was talking to me, presumably, but he looked straight ahead out of his windscreen. Ettie, I think about you all the time, he said.

He looked ashamed then and he stared at the steering wheel; then he hit it hard with both his hands.

Look, do you want to or not? he said.

I looked outwards, to the different distances of dark blue in the valley around us.

Then I looked back at Aaron, at his dark profile.

Yeah, alright, I said. I do.

Aaron was almost instantly on top of me. My skirt ruched up. I felt a slight rush and I concentrated on it. I closed my eyes. I let my head fall backwards, to constrict my throat. But I couldn't get the breathing quite right. I opened my eyes and I gripped the sides of the car seat. I focussed on the outline of the hilltops right over on the other side of the valley as Aaron moved against me.

These hills were once on the same latitude as the Port of Sudan and Santiago de Cuba. Mr Holmes, with his long face and his desperately sad eyes, had told us this in Geography lessons. He talked a lot about the valley. *You could once have walked on land all the way from the Flower Scar to the South Pole,* he'd told us. *Way back in deep time, hundreds of millions of years ago, the world was one enormous landmass, a Pangaea, surrounded by sea. The land slowly, slowly, broke apart, drifting into the continents we now know. Of all the cycles of the earth—the seasons, the tides, night and day—this is the most dramatic. The earth is pulling apart. And one day, in hundreds more millions of years, the continents will collide again. They'll recombine to make a supercontinent, and the shape of this new world will be totally unrecognisable.*

No one seemed to listen to Mr Holmes but me: I loved his descriptions of the earth moving. Stacey was writing notes next to me in class as he spoke: *Do you think Holmes is depressed? Chan says he keeps booze in the stationary cupboard. Ettie, I'm bored!!!* But I ignored her. When I let myself go entirely, when I played dead in the dark, I could sometimes feel it, that slow violent tremor through the ground below me. Through the ground that had swallowed her and would one day swallow me.

Aaron was moving more and more quickly. I closed my eyes again. I hyperventilated, quietly, so that Aaron wouldn't hear. I was just beginning to go when Aaron collapsed on top of me. He ugged, and then he reared up, before dropping himself heavily back into the driver's seat. He fixed his clothes, he cleared his throat, and then he opened the window onto the cool night sky and he spat out into it.

Four

On my seventeenth birthday, Aaron took me for a drive and proposed to me. I laughed. I couldn't help it. He snatched the ring-box back into his pocket and looked at me for a moment in bleak confusion, before telling me to get out of the car. I spent that evening walking home along the side of the bypass. And after that, Aaron stopped driving me up onto the tops. He said I must have some sort of altitude sickness, with all the dizziness. Sometimes I'd pass out too soon, before he got properly going, and he'd get angry and tell me to stop playing silly beggars. *Just stay conscious, Ettie*, he'd say. *It's not right. I can't do it if you're not conscious.*

Most nights, I was alone in the house again. Dad worked even later hours. I worked in the evenings too, revising for my exams. I would memorise essay points and then I would lie back on my bed, holding my breath in the dark, listening to the house creak, drifting in and out of consciousness. When I did well in my A-levels, everyone seemed surprised. But I loved reading poetry in the evenings before I passed out. Perhaps the de-oxygenation had made me especially receptive to Keats's visions *more strange, and strange, and dim, And then were gulfed in tumultuous swim*; to Joyce's version of *some new world, fantastic, dim, uncertain as under sea*. Sometimes

I thought I felt her drawing close—my mother, Moira—as I recited the words and arched my body upwards. As I let my head fall backwards, I felt her as a shiver through my spine.

I'd been offered a place at Leeds to study English Literature. I would live at home to save on expense, my dad told me. So once I'd passed my exams, I made the journey across to Leeds several times a week, taking the train that cut through the bottom of the valley and sped its landscape past me. There was a boy on my course, Rufus, who smelled of hemp and mouldering grass. He sat next to me in Introduction to Poetics seminars, and he often lolloped alongside me afterwards, trying to get me to delay the journey back to Todmorden and come to the pub. We sometimes sat together in the Dry Dock, a beached barge-turned-bar in the middle of the ring road, drinking bitter and making jokes. Rufus betrayed his background almost immediately despite his ambient odour and crumpled appearance: he had been educated at Harrow and his parents were academics. Rufus would tell me about his agonising holidays back home from school, when his every word was noted by his parents. He was convinced they were chalking it all up for later discussion and analysis. He told me that he became almost silent, for a while, fearing their scrutiny. In seminars, he often blushed deeply when he spoke, his sonorous voice seeming to resound against his will.

In our final year, Rufus invited me to move into a squatted house in Chapel Allerton. I didn't tell Dad all the details, but he still didn't want me to go. It would just be for a year, I told him, and I barely saw my father at home anyway. I persuaded him that I needed to be learning to live out in the world, and he finally agreed to me going. The Cherry Street squat was well-organised. There were grilles on the front windows, so the light came in in perforations, but otherwise it was perfectly homely. The couple who had cracked the house open slept in the living room. They were Bradford anarchists who lived on food recovered from supermarket skips. Each evening they used to go out into Leeds, kitted out like renegade poachers: khaki jackets, combats, netted bags, adrenaline-readied to leap walls and dangle over the edge of massive food bins, fishing for deformed bagels and use-by expired mackerel. They would bring back their cache and improvise exquisite meals: trout with poached eggs and roasted beetroot; pork with bruised peaches and goat's cheese; serrano ham and celeriac hash; all washed down with a Chablis shoplifted from the Tesco Metro. In what might once have been the dining room lived a Danish journalist, Begitte, who wrote about the evils of the capitalist property market and the ethical necessity of squatting. She spoke several languages fluently and lived almost entirely on raw food. Upstairs was Rufus's room, which was filled with books and photographs and records, and the occasional beautiful girl draped over his furniture. Next to him was a box-room where Jay, a near-silent heroin addict, slept in a methadone swoon. And across the hall from them was what would become my room.

When I arrived, a brutal-looking dog stood guarding the door: a pit-bull cross, black with a white patch across one eye and shoulders that were wider than mine. Rufus ruffled the dog's ears, in a not altogether convincing way.

It's Jay's dog. The house dog now, I suppose, Rufus said. Jay doesn't really get out to walk him, so we take him out when we can. Good boy, Braxus.

The dog pushed its enormous head against my thigh and whined. I nudged my way past it.

My room was at the back of the house, so there were no grilles on the windows. The roof sloped down to a mattress against the back wall. The walls were painted orange and the room smelled of wood. I loved it. For almost a year, I slept and read and drank and passed out in that room, looking out on the cherry trees on the back street and listening to Peter Green's Fleetwood Mac on repeat. Aaron came across to visit me a couple of times. We still saw each other every once in a while. Leanne had told me he was waiting for me *to sort myself out*. He brought round buckets of fried chicken, and told me it wasn't right, living like this. He could apply for a mortgage now, he said. He had a deposit and proof of earnings. I could move in with him and live somewhere half-decent. They were doing a shared ownership scheme at Bailey Bridge. Didn't I want to get away from living like this?

On weekends, I used to go dancing with Rufus and I ingested anything and everything that was offered to me. This seemed like good manners. We used to go to the West Indian Centre and listen to dub so loud that I could feel my internal organs palpitate at their different resonating frequencies. Sometimes this would be too much of a temptation. I'd begin to let go in the bobbing frenzy of dreadlocks and sweat and adrenaline. I'd close my eyes and begin to search for the green lights behind them. And then I'd begin to go; I'd feel the swoop in my stomach and everything would go wonderfully blurry.

But Rufus got sick of the bouncers forcing him to take me outside. He said I needed to learn my limits. And he invited me out less and less often.

During the week, I would read and read, and Braxus would loll with his massive head on my lap, drooling on my knees as I worked my way through two centuries of haunted novels. The pace at which I read was ferocious. But I retained next to nothing. It began to feel like the words were so much water running through my brain; nothing of it remained, but it flowed on through, and that flow felt as though it might be keeping me alive.

The more I read, the worse I did in my exams and essays.

I'd brought the cashmere blanket from my mother's old room with me to Leeds, and I kept it under my pillow. My talent was well-developed. I would begin by caressing the cashmere, feeling its softness against my skin. Then I would lean back and close my eyes. The light from outside would gleam against my closed eyelids, pulsing and phosphores-cent. Sometimes I tried to hear the music; sometimes I even played the music: the screech of the violins, the pooling, overwhelming swell. And I would arch my spine, letting my head fall all the way back to constrict my throat. Sometimes I would hang off the edge of the bed, dangling my head upside down. On a good day, everything would soften instantly at the edges, and I'd feel her drawing close before I went under. On a bad day, I'd pass out too quickly, and I'd splutter back to life with Braxus licking my cheeks.

In the spring, things at the squat started to get agitated. There were rallies in town against the privatisation of higher education and Rufus and the anarchists joined an occupa-tion of the University's buildings. I tagged along with Rufus to meetings and marched alongside him in a demonstration. I let my body get crushed into the bodies of the other people there. The way a woman's shoulder pushed right up against mine, again and again, and the woman didn't even notice, or if she did, she let it carry on—it made me feel dizzy. I spent a couple of broken nights sleeping on the floor of a conference centre, where I breathed in the carpet dust and listened to people chatting on the balcony and playing guitar through the night. Rufus knew everyone in the movement—in fact he'd slept with most of the girls. He often spoke at length in the group discussions, while people sat round in a circle using occult hand-signals. Rufus's face bloomed whenever he orated; he looked truly happy. Other people seemed to instantly trust him by his blush. Writers, academics and broadcasters sent their solidarity and came to give talks in the evenings. People baked us cakes and braved the University's security staff to deliver them. And it turned out that Rufus was well-connected: journalists, professors, past MPs, all came to address us at his invitation. The real coup was Rufus's godfather: H.E. Bell would launch his new poetry collection, with attendant publicity, from the sit-in.

Bell arrived at the occupation with a terrified-looking publisher, and wandered round the space, talking to the great unwashed with evident pleasure. He was an enormous man: six-foot-six and broad across the shoulders, but narrowed to nothing in his waist and the pits of his cheeks. He wore a velvet jacket and a cravat, and had a booming, patrician voice. On the night of his reading, hundreds crushed into the occupation space. Rufus gave out specific directions in the case of a fire, because the University had blocked our fire escapes. Someone from the crowd shouted, *Corporate murder*, and everyone cheered. Bell began with a long address on poetry and political action. He told us that acts of resistance were works of art. He told us that the fight began here, that we must carry it on to save education and the hope of a more egalitarian society. We must resist the changes that had been made since the Browne Review, and the invasion of the neo-liberal body snatchers. And then he read his new poems to rapturous applause.

Afterwards, Bell's editor hovered at a desk with his books set out, and Bell held court, signing copies and clapping occupiers on the back. Rufus produced a bottle of cava and we toasted the new collection with plastic cups. There was something unsettling about the way Bell kept looking at me. When people asked him questions, about his poetry, or his politics, he had a way of shutting them down with a joke, or of humouring them but letting everyone else see how basic the question was. The evening wore on. Someone brought Bell a chair. Students circled him. He stared wildly at each one as they spoke. His nostrils flared. He snorted unabashedly at some comments. And his eyes keep lighting on me; he looked down his nose, as though sighting me down the barrel of a gun. Rufus laughed horribly loudly at everything he said. The publisher had sold all the books and was beginning to ready Bell for his departure. Everyone wanted to shake his hand before he left. As he made his way past me, he swooped suddenly, and grabbed me hard by the upper arm:

'Meet me outside in ten minutes, little girl,' he said. 'I'd like to give you something.'

He dropped my arm just as suddenly and shook more hands on his way out.

I curled up in a corner. I watched the main occupation leaders at the front of the room making plans for the next day, deciding who to invite for the Friday-night slot. Two of them knew famous comedians and the group was now arguing about which of the two was the least problematic and who would draw the largest crowd. I wanted to leave. But I didn't want to see what it was that Bell wanted to *give me*. I spent a few more hours there in the occupation, and then, when it was safe, I ventured back out into the city.

I stayed away from the action after that. I spent a lot of time in my room. I read and I wrote during the day. I drank and I passed out in the evenings. The nights were getting warmer. The sky was brightening. One evening in May, I was walking back along Cherry Street with a stack of books, breathing in the smell of lit pollen and beer that was rising from the students on their front steps. When I arrived at our front door, a police officer was barring the way.

Do you live here? the woman asked. Her voice was kind, despite her bearing.

Yes, I said. Sort of.

Then we're going to need to ask you some questions, she said.

Another officer ushered me through to the kitchen and asked me to sit down. The other doors were shut, but I could hear footsteps in the room above—in my room. And the house smelled strange: some new addition, a hint of metal and salt.

The officer explained to me, slowly and in deliberately simple terms, the outline of what had happened, with timings and locations cross-referenced against his note-book. I elaborated the scene in my mind as the officer stirred sugar into a cup of tea for me that would apparently help with the shock. Begitte had raised the alarm at 15.07. She had been working at her desk that afternoon, researching an article. Seemingly out of nowhere, a small orb of bright liquid had dropped onto her page. It had spread

28

into a bright orange circle on the paper, working its way through the grain. And then another drop had followed. And then another. Begitte had looked up. A livid patch of reddish brown was bleeding across the ceiling above her, a bright, asymmetric bulge of colour either side of a line in the plasterboard. It was darkest at the centre, spreading to bright orange at the edges, as though the plasterboard were litmus. She had no idea what it could be. A break in a pipe that was full of liquid rust? A psychedelic attack of liquid legionnaires?

Exsanguinated. That was the word. I wanted to give the officer the word. Perhaps he didn't know it? It pooled in my mouth, unspoken. Exsanguinated. The fatal loss of blood from the body. Jay had slit his wrists. And he'd done it properly, scoring vertically along from the tender crux-points behind the elbow all the way to his wrists. He had slumped against the wall and bled his way out into the floorboards, bleeding along the joists, through the plasterboard, and down onto Begitte's white page.

I'm afraid we recovered some drugs paraphernalia in your friend's room. So we need to conduct a search of the rest of the property, the police officer told me.

Where's Braxus? I asked.

Braxus? the policeman echoed.

The dog. Jay's dog.

The policeman looked at his notes.

We did discover a dog at the property, he said. But I'm afraid it had to be confiscated under the Dangerous Dogs Act.

Confiscated?

The dog is illegal, he said. It will need to be destroyed.

When the police had finished their search of my room, I retrieved the cashmere blanket and left most of my other things behind me. I walked back down the pollen-filled street towards town. I took the train to Todmorden and walked back along the canal path. It was a soft, warm evening. I knocked at the front door of the lock-keeper's cottage. My father had Wagner on in the living room and had unbuttoned his shirt. He looked half-cut.

Esther, he said, staring at me. Whatever have you done to yourself?

He opened the door and then stood watching as I walked back up the stairs to my old room.

Five

For a year, I stayed at the bottom of the valley. I signed on, and then got a job delivering free magazines for a marketing company in Halifax, and then they bumped me up to proof-reading. I'd go out on work nights and smoke spliffs in pub car parks and occasionally get off with one of the lads who worked in the office. I could turn myself out like a light now; I did it in the loos on my breaks from work; I did it on the bus journey home. But there was no one to appreciate my talent.

Dad said I needed to have more ambition. That I had a degree, which was more than he'd ever had, no matter the classification. He drove me down to London at the start of the summer—we sped down the M1, and then into the intestinal streets of the city. In the last stages of the journey, the car moved slowly along a road in south London and a heat-haze streamed upwards from the stationary traffic ahead of us, making zigzags of fumes on the air. I'd been to London once as a child; she brought me here one Christmas to see *The Nutcracker*. But this looked nothing like my memories of Covent Garden. I stared out of the open car window, watching the procession of people on the pavement. White boys with mean, thin bodies were strutting, shirtless, on a garage forecourt. One of them yanked a squat dog on a lead that had been improvised from string. A gang of children jostled for position outside a newsagent, smoking and competitively swearing. Tables lined the pavement in front of shops, offering up boxes full of mangoes and arthritic-looking vegetables. In the windows, naked halal chickens hung by the score.

What do you think of it, then? Dad asked as the car crawled down the high street.

I didn't say anything. But I was excited. From the paranoid look of the men gathered outside the mobile-phone shop, to the unfeasibly pink pool of freshly ejected sick at the end of my new street, to the violent movement of people and vehicles in every direction: it was a completely new scene.

Dad, I said, turn here. This is it.

We drove down Marlborough Road, past the white facades of the Victorian terraces, and pulled up at number 29. I had very little with me. On the back seat of my father's car sat a carrier bag with some shoes in it, two carrier bags full of clothes and bedding, another carrier bag of cosmetics, and a final carrier bag with some of her things. I gathered these together and then stood with Dad on the doorstep. He rang the bell. The house had a small front garden. Two overgrown rose bushes were coming into bloom. A climber, desiccated, twisted over the door and up the front of the house.

We heard heavy footfall on the stairs inside, and then my cousin appeared at the door.

Hello. Esther. Uncle Vince. Veronica raised her right hand. She didn't smile exactly. She stood for a moment on the threshold, eyeing me up, as though she might have thought better of the whole thing. But then she ushered us inside, towards the kitchen at the back of the house.

The Lost Art of Sinking

Dad leant against a worktop, testing surfaces with a tap of his nails, like a covert surveyor. I stood close to him, still clutching my carrier bags. I wasn't sure if I should make myself at home just yet.

Veronica put the kettle on and asked us about our journey. Veronica was a junior doctor. She has always been a solid person, certain of her usefulness to the world and socially at ease. I remembered a childhood family trip to a stately home outside Peterborough where we'd met my aunt and uncle and Vron. I had sloped off with her, thinking we were drawn together into a cousinly conspiracy, and then she had forced me to climb a tree, standing below me with a long, sharp stick and pricking my thighs whenever I stopped moving. This, Veronica had said, was to toughen me up.

Listen, Esther, make yourself at home, Veronica said. I've got to dash to a shift, but I've had these keys cut for you, and your room's right at the top. Sorry I can't stay, old man. She batted Dad on the arm. Duty calls, she said, and then she was out through the front door.

I liked my new room. It reminded me of the squat, because of the slope of the roof, and the smell of wood. It only took me a few minutes to unpack. I folded Mum's cashmere blanket under my pillow. I came back downstairs to find my father poking about in the kitchen. There were stacks of crockery around the sink, and half-eaten things had been abandoned on the worktops. There was a distinct smell of mouse.

This is how the other half lives, eh? Dad said. He emitted a short laugh. I'll take you out for dinner before I head back, love.

We set off on foot back towards the main road, walking through through the warm petrol evening. At the end of the road, a man was sitting on the ground, against the wall of a Cambodian takeaway and fish-and-chip shop. He was sweating. He was wearing a filthy wax jacket. He had ejected another puddle of vomit. Dad upped the pace towards Tooting.

We opted for a Sri Lankan restaurant, with bamboo place mats. We ordered too much food; Dad was being beneficent. He told to me to dig in, but I could see he was slightly horrified when I kept on going. I downed four large bottles of lager and then I ordered us spirits. He was studying my face: my lurid orange lipstick, which had probably smudged. It sometimes left a bright wax on my teeth. My hair, which was a dull mink colour, hung heavily around my face. I know that when I don't wear mascara, my eyes look derelict. I could see that Dad was finding it painful to appraise my face. He'd like me to be well-groomed—like she was.

Will you go for the job then, love? It's tomorrow morning, remember, ten a.m.

Dad had got me the chance of an interview for a temp receptionist job at a paper in north London, where he used to work.

You won't have to do something so menial for long, I'm sure. They're bound to promote you, he said.

It sounds good, I said. I'll go to the interview.

I downed my final drink, and then we headed back towards Veronica's house. We stopped at a crossing on the main road and Dad pressed the button. Cars and motorbikes sped past, relentless even on a Sunday evening.

Just a minute, I said. I felt a little peculiar. I thought I might be about to spontaneously pass out; that had never happened before. Perhaps it would be a sign of some kind? But instead, I held on to the crossing post, turned myself a half circle around it, and bent over the gutter. As the green man started beeping, I threw up my entire meal into the road.

Oh, Esther, love. Dad bent down to help me. Esther. I'm not sure I should leave you here.

I reared back up, laughing. Don't be soft, Dad, I said.

I spat into the gutter, and then linked his arm, zigzagging him all the way back to the house.

It took ages to get rid of him. We searched out coffee in the cupboards, and once this was finished, nothing could legitimately delay him.

As he stood on the doorstep, he caught me by the wrist.

Let me see your eyes, love, he said.

He caught my chin and tilted my face up towards his.

He was doing this to try to see *her*, I knew. Because our eyes are the same strange colour. A milky grey that she called violet.

He let go of my chin.

Esther, London's a big place, he said. It's different from home. You have to be careful.

He sniffed hard and pushed his thumb and forefinger into his eyelids.

I stared up at the sky. He was making me remember the night of Mum's funeral when, after everyone else had gone, I was left in the front room with Dad. A new family of two. He had been drinking enough to make him weepy. He had taken my hand. *Esther*, he had said staring into the fireplace. *Esther, I sometimes have the strangest thoughts. It's only that I want to protect you. I tried to protect your mother...* And then he had dropped my hand, and leant back into the sofa, pressing his thumbs into his eyes.

You've got a long journey ahead, Dad, I said. It's getting late.

Yes, he said. You're right. I'll go.

He kissed me, and then he moved away down the path. At the gate he turned back towards me.

I've tried my best, Esther, he said, even if...

He couldn't finish the sentence.

Drive safe, Dad, I said, and I closed the door.

I ran straight up to my new room, in the eaves, and opened the skylight, letting in the warm night air. I lay on the bed, listening for the sound of my father's car pulling away.

I thought of her then, and I pushed my face into the cashmere blanket and started to hyperventilate.

When I was very young, on Sunday nights we sometimes drove back along the motorway from my Nana's house in Doncaster. I would look out into the blackness and see the squares of light from houses in nearby towns. It was such a strange thought, that there were all these people, inside their homes, eating their teas and making jokes and sitting on their sofas, who knew nothing about us, who didn't know about my exquisitely beautiful mother, and would never know that we had been there, secretly in the dark, speeding past them, seeing their windows and wondering about them.

And now, lying in my new bed, I thought of all the people in London, living in parallel, their rooftops multiplying away towards the city centre. I was thinking that, in the overwhelming majority, they would never know, or even wonder about me. I could chalk them up as parallel lines on a wall, and they would repeat away, exceeding my ability to mark them, because of all the new people being born. And even though I couldn't count them, we were all in the city together, at the same time, duplicating one another. I was joining them, just as she had before me; all out bodies were in parallel. I sank further into the bed and let myself go right under. When I slept, I dreamt of falling.

Six

I found a tube map in the back of Veronica's *A to Z* and, the next morning, I took the black line for the very first time. The tube felt like an old fairground ride of the kind that you shouldn't trust: it pulled away from each station, judderingly and with effort at first, up the ascent, then gaining speed and hurtling down to the next stop. I marvelled at each station as a seemingly-fit-to-burst carriage squeezed in an extra couple of people. It reminded me of Dad's old party trick: he would slip five-pence pieces into an already brimming pint, squeezing the metal discs down the inside of the glass, the ale rising to a dome in the middle as more and more pieces were artfully eased in, seeming to defy the laws of space. Sitting opposite me, an older woman in festival-bright lycras, staring ahead and out of the window at the furred black insides of the tube tunnel. Diagonally opposite: a smartly dressed young woman with a severe chignon. Next to her, a jaundiced looking man, sweat puckering on his upper lip as he stares intently at the woman's ballet pumps.

I changed onto the grey line at London Bridge, as did many of the same passengers. We moved like a school of fish through the station tunnels and took our places in a new carriage. A couple of moments in, and a strong smell prickled my nostrils. I thought at first that a dog must have squeezed its way onto the tube between the legs of the passengers. I glanced in the direction of the odour: a large man in a high-vis jacket was pushing his way towards me to catch hold of a pole. His hair was lank and his chin was stubbled. When he stood right in front of me, I could practically see the smell coming off of him. A woman standing nearby turned her head away. Another put a handkerchief across her face. No one could escape that smell though. I settled into my seat and began to breathe deeply. I let my head fall backwards. I closed my eyes and concentrated. The odour was waxy at first, like lanolin and ears and dirty scalps. And then it stung into something more vinegary and sharply testicular. I breathed in again. Finally the smell tanged into mouldering yeast. The man's body was impressing itself on everyone in the carriage. It was obscene. The more I breathed, the stronger the smell became. He was blooming in my nose. Wet dog and cider-groin and thickened scalp-fat hit me hard in the sinuses. I thought about my first London swoon being here, on the Underground. But then I started to gag and Swiss Cottage was announced.

The newspaper building was glass fronted and the sunshine made the grain of the white-marble floor sparkle. It was much grander than anywhere I had imagined temping. People surged into the foyer around me, breasting up out of the tube and on through the building.

I approached the front desk.

Hello, I said, I'm Esther Freestone. I'm here about the receptionist role.

The Lost Art of Sinking

Oh, here she is then, said the woman on the other side of the desk, who stood to the right of a flower arrangement with a pineapple as its centrepiece.

I'm supposed to tell you that the job's yours, she said. This is your seat. You start today.

She motioned towards the chair at the side of her.

Oh, I said. Okay, I wasn't... I thought it was just an interview today? But... right. Thank you?

I made my way round the reception. On my side of the desk there was a computer, a piece of paper with log-in details, an empty desk-tidy, a company mug full of biros. I sat down on the spin chair and plummeted down a few inches.

Yes, your chair can be a little... unpredictable, the woman said. *Polly* never minded it.

She looked straight ahead at her screen and jabbed at her keyboard, her fingernails clack-clacking. The movement was so fast and aggressive that it was difficult to believe she was typing into a real document. On her side of the desk there was: another company mug, this one with a red-brown lipstick pucker on the rim; a photograph of an older man, stood amongst racing dogs; two paperweights, identical except for the colour of the swirls inside; a packet of Silk Cuts; a small mound of multicoloured paperclips; and a name plate: Maureen Gibson.

You've got some forms to sign and a safety video to watch for the next hour, Maureen said. If you don't get a move on to HR you'll be late for it.

I sat alone in a room without windows. The room had shelving on each wall, and each shelf held of packets of paper and envelopes and pens. It was in truth a large stationery cupboard in which someone had set up a TV. A woman from HR had introduced herself earlier and provided a plastic seat for me. She turned off the lights and made a joke about popcorn. Then I sat in the dark and watched a man on the screen lifting things off a pallet—in the right way (*knees bent: big green tick*); and in the wrong way (*bending from the hips: enormous red cross*). For a moment I wondered what on earth I was doing here in this cupboard in north London. But then I sank into the dark, and let my head fall backwards. I didn't go completely. Just enough to remind me that she had once been here, in this city, too. Just enough to feel her through the shiver in my spine.

The brightness of the foyer was startling after the cupboard. Maureen barely acknowledged my return. We sat mostly in silence for the rest of the day. Maureen had provided a thick, printed guide to various telephony and online systems for me to read.

At six o'clock Maureen turned on me suddenly, with a look of some violence.

Right, she said, we're taking you to the pub.

I shut down my computer and followed her out of the building.

Maureen lit up as we stood on the edge of the busy main road. We were going to *The Swiss*, Maureen informed me. Maureen's mouth squeezed repeatedly in a tight, bright-brown anus around the end of her fag as we waited to cross. The Swiss Cottage pub was directly opposite the office, marooned on an island in the middle of the traffic. There were four lanes either side, and the noise was enormous.

Once we'd crossed, Maureen took a seat at a picnic table;

its legs were concreted into an entirely grey area that was signposted, *Beer Garden.*

I'll have a white-wine soda, Maureen said, and pointed towards the door.

Stepping inside the pub was like stepping into another season: the tiny windows let in very little light. Several old men sat at the bar, red-nosed, and one nodded at me, swilling his glass. There was an old woman, hunched like a boulder, next to an empty fireplace, guarding a tartan wheel-along shopping trolley and a tiny dog. A man with a sports bag full of knock-off DVDs wound his way from table to table. Two women stood like henges behind the bar, both of them skinny with blanched faces and gothic lipstick, moving to pull pints when called.

I bought the drinks and went back out to the blue sky and car fumes. I sat down next to Maureen and we sank into an uncompanionable silence.

Maureen gulped back her drink and chain-smoked.

It's warm, no, she said after a while.

Some men from the office sat down on a table behind us and Maureen leaned back, pushing into their conversation, asking how they all were, roaring with laughter at their jokes.

I'll have a white-wine soda, ta, she said to one of the men, as he got up to go to the bar.

At some point late on in the evening, when all the picnic tables were full and the separate parties had spilled over into one another, a man sat down next to me.

You look a bit lost, he said. He had sandy hair, and a sandy face: tan, rough, a gold-blond greying beard. He was older than me, and his voice lilted upwards, towards the North-East.

Oh, I'm just new here, I said. My first day, in fact.

Is that so? he said. Do you work at the paper?

Yeah, I said. I'm just a temp. And then, to be charming and whimsical, I offered: It's a bit like being on a ship here, isn't it?

How do you mean? he said.

This pub, I said. We're on the deck, at the prow. I gesticulated with my glass. And that roar of the road rushing around us is the sea, I said.

He looked at me like I might be deranged. I could see him assessing the situation, deciding whether I was too drunk to pursue.

He knocked back his pint.

Yeah, he said, yeah, I can see what you mean. If, that is, you mean the North Sea—brimming with pollution and discarded condoms and the ghosts of lost souls.

My laugh seemed to vaporise in the warm night. The sky had sunk to navy blue above and around us, and the black tower blocks across the road were now a faraway shore.

Can I buy you a drink? he asked.

When he got back, he started telling me about real boats, and his childhood growing up on a quayside. He was called Tom. I wanted to talk to him more. In truth, I thought he might be a good first-night audience.

We've missed the last tube, he said. Whatever shall we do?

We lay in an enormous bed in a serviced apartment. Thomas had begged the key from a friend who was working the desk of the town-house hotel just a ten-minute walk away in Belsize Park. The friend had given him a look like, *What, again, mate?* But then he'd smirked and handed the key over.

The Lost Art of Sinking

We made a post-coital V in that big raft of a bed, our feet touching. As dawn broke over London and spilled in through the blinds, I told Tom him about the valley—about Ted Hughes' Crow and UFOs and the fact that the place name, *Todmorden*, is, by some accounts, derived from 'tod', meaning death, and 'mort', meaning death, making it *death-death-wood*. I asked Thomas to tell me more about the place he'd grown up. And as I drew his stories out, I let my breathing quicken.

Thomas grew up on the Wear at the edge of a Sunderland shipyard in a terrace of houses at the very limit of the land. Back when he was small, when they were shipbuilding, steamers would grow up right in front of his front door: thirty feet behind their television set, the newest ship would rise straight up, a sheer cliff of steel. The house would be dark for months. And then, on the day of the launch, a freighter's horn would blast, and the new ship would be off: sunshine would flood their house again.

Every so often, at night, Thomas and his sister would wake to the siren's scream: they would peer out of the curtains, two tiny ghouls, to watch the searchlight's beam circle across the surface of the dark water.

Thomas's father had been black trade—a welder. He was an incomer, down from Scotland, and he hated the yards. And that was before they knew about the worst of the risks, too: how the muck they brought home wasn't just so much oil worked into carpets and creases of skin, but trails of poison. Thomas told me how he now imagined it: the asbestos arcing through their house from the tips of his father's fingers. And he told me he often thought that poison must be settled at

45

the bottom of his lungs, waiting there. Silicosis and asbestosis had spread through all of the workers' families.

I held myself right at the edge, just between dizziness and passing out, as he told me all this.

When things at the yard got difficult, he said, his parents started to argue. His father's work was dwindling. His mother had grown up in the yards—her father had worked them through the war years, when Sunderland made a quarter of the tonnage of all of the ships. Sunderland had won the Second World War, Thomas's grandfather always said to him. And his grandad had vowed he'd build ships until he died—which he did, at fifty-five years old, when a piece of ironstone fell out of a bucket swinging above his head and shattered his skull.

Their yard was the last to shut finally in 1988. Nothing worse than those ships, Thomas told me, except for them being gone.

Their house was light all the time now, but the light was eerily bright, carrying seagull cries through the silence into the living room. The quay was deserted. And at night, instead of the scream of the siren, he and his sister would wake to the sound of drunken men raging at the water.

After the yard's closure, his mother, Mary, stayed in her room a lot. And then his father, Mick, left them and moved to the south, for new work and a new family. Mick would come back up, every so often, and sit in his car outside the house, waiting to take Thomas's sister out for her visit. He would take Amanda out for the day, and she would come back home with ridiculous presents. They had no money for school dinners or shoes, but Amanda had new earrings and a ring with a pink, cut-glass stone. After a while Thomas stopped hoping for his own visit. His mother didn't do much around the house now; she lived on meal replacement drinks, switching to gin in the evenings. She bought in biscuits and cereal for Thomas and his sister. Amanda was desperate to get away, so he tried to keep the house together as best he could to keep her at home. He learned to cook: by the time he was twelve he could do a mean vindaloo, with lemon-meringue pie for afters. He would persuade his sister to invite her friends over for tea. He made lasagne and shepherd's pie and corned-beef hash, all out of his paper-round money. His mother sneered and said he had no real skills, not like his grandfather, or his father. But his sister and her mates crowded round most evenings, calling him a proper little chef, sometimes kissing him full on the lips and then laughing in his face.

Still, though, his sister wanted to leave. And as soon as she was sixteen, Amanda came down to London. She danced in clubs, she said in a postcard with Beefeaters on the front, and was drinking a lot of champagne. She lived in a flat in Hampstead owned by a very rich man, who was in love with her. Their mother tore the postcard into four uneven squares and put them in the bin. Thomas decided that as soon as he was able, he would follow Amanda. He saved his odd-job money and, at fifteen, took the coach down to London Victoria. But when he got to Mandy's flat it was not what he had expected: there were four girls sharing a bedroom, sleeping on two stained double mattresses on the floor, and when the man who owned the flat came round, Amanda made him hide in a wardrobe. He hated it there, and his sister looked tired and sallow. But she swore blind she wouldn't go back home. Thomas spent a couple of weeks sleeping rough on benches on Hampstead Heath. Then he got a job at a crêperie and spent the next twenty years working his way through various hotel kitchens in north London. He managed a coffee shop now, he told me—it was all bought-in cheesecake and frappuccinos. And as he aerated hot milk, he sometimes wondered where the time had gone, and how big the dark sparks in his lungs had grown.

Thomas turned over to face me when he'd finished talking. I could feel his eyes on me. I arched my body and cut off my breath.

I felt a shiver through my spine. I started to slide into unconsciousness.

What are you doing? he said, and he shook me. What the fuck? What is this? Is this what you get off on? Fucking hell. Stop it.

The morning was muggy. The warm air was close about me as I trailed down the Finchley Road towards the office. I was near delirious from lack of sleep. When I sat down behind the reception desk, it was 9.03. Maureen looked over at me and made a clicking sound with her tongue. As everyone streamed into work, as I put through calls and booked rooms for meetings, I let Thomas's stories circle in my mind. And something else was circling in my thoughts too. It was the indulgent weariness in the eyes of the man at the hotel desk the night before as he handed Thomas the keys to the apartment. A look that suggested Thomas's incorrigibility. Our evening was one of many. Thomas's request for the keys to an empty room must been repeated at least enough times to produce that weariness in his friend. My body in that bed, alongside Thomas's, was just one part of a series of repetitions. Thinking of this started to make me properly dizzy.

From behind the reception desk, 1 could see the sky above north London becoming dark as a bruise. Each besuited visitor drove humid air in through the revolving doors, and it began to smell warm and animal in the foyer.

1 thought of the city circling close around me, and around Thomas, and around all the other bodies that had preceded and would replace me.

And 1 thought of her—of course 1 did—1 felt her as the hairs rose on my arms and the storm broke in forks of light through the violet sky.

Seven

A month in London, and there'd been no spectacular show. I'd had high hopes of the tube at first. The black line tunnelled me home each day and the further south we got, the hotter it seemed to be, as though we were travelling deeper into the earth. The heat helped to make me dizzy and there was certainly a captive audience. I often let myself blur into a semi-conscious state by the time we got to Clapham—but so did plenty of other commuters.

It rained and rained that summer. One evening, when I re-emerged above ground in Colliers Wood, it was sheeting down. My shoes filled with water and when I turned off the high street, the pavement was littered with snails.

Inside number 29, Veronica was sitting at the kitchen table, eating toast and poring over some papers.

You're squelching, she said, without looking up, as I came into the kitchen.

Yes, I said. It's raining.

Vron crunched her toast and didn't look at me.

I don't know where you're going to, Ettie, she said, at night. And I honestly don't care. But I've got your dad breathing down my neck, and my dad, and I'm supposed to make sure you don't go *off the rails*, aren't I?

I sat down. I could feel the water make a skein around my buttocks on the wooden seat. The previous night, I had met Thomas again and we had gone back to the same serviced apartment. But he didn't want to talk about his family this time, and he was on me so quick I didn't have time to hyperventilate.

I don't know why anyone's on at you, I said. I'm going to work every day. I'm earning my keep, aren't I? I'll be able to give you rent at the end of this month.

As a temp on reception? Is that what you really want to do? Vron looked up at me then.

I imagine I looked fairly pitiful, with my hair plastered to my cheeks.

It's easy to feel superfluous around Veronica. Vron is such a real and solid person.

No wonder you're going out and getting... whatever it is, she said to me. You must be bored out of your skull there. Look, Ettie, she said to me, why don't you think about doing something at the hospital? We need good people. The phlebotomy ward is desperate, in fact, and they'll train you on the job. If you had a skill like that, you could be *really* useful, here or anywhere else in the world. She pushed the last corner of toast into her mouth. At least think about it, Ettie, she said. I could take you in to shadow someone.

Phlebotomy? I asked. Isn't that blood?

Yes, she said. It would mean working with blood. You'd be collecting blood samples for testing. You'd get over any initial queasiness. Everyone does after a bit.

I'll think about it, I said. For sure.

Vron grabbed her rucksack and moved away towards the door.

I've got a shift, she said. There's leftover lasagne in the fridge.

That evening I lay on my bed, beneath the skylight, and thought again about the remainder of my night with Thomas. It wasn't that late when we'd finished our drinks. We hadn't missed the last tube. But Thomas had insisted, again, that we go to the hotel in Belsize Park, rather than to his flat. And his face had become over-animated when he said it. Aggressively jokey. Panicky.

There was someone at home. He must have someone at home.

I felt, again, that dizzying sense of my repeatability. It was almost enough to send me under.

I lay still for a while, watching bits of glittering far-away fire in the sky through the rain-grubbed glass of the skylight.

And then I had an idea.

If you really want to get to know this city, Maureen had once said to me, with a mean taunt in her voice. *You want to try online dating. You'll get to see what it's like out there then.*

I stole back down to the kitchen. Veronica's laptop was on the table. I huddled it upstairs with me. I fired it up: no password needed. I opened the internet and typed in *London dating*. Myriad links replicated down the screen. I clicked on the first one.

There were faces. So many faces. Head shots of grinning girls.

I began to feel a slight shiver.

I steadied myself, to hold it off, and started, slowly, to breathe more deeply.

Small rectangles with white borders repeated themselves

down the left-hand side of the screen, displaying decapitated female heads. Glittering eyes, cheeks pushed up, top lips making strange, inviting shapes. There was text in the box next to each head. The pseudonyms appeared in the largest text: *Just_one_dimple / Sinequanon / Geeky_Redhead / Quirky_English_Rose / Funky_gibbon / Lost in translation / Opal74 / Piscean78/ Pepper81 / Rumi76 / Indigo_79 / Helen_of_ Troy / Superwoman / ModernMarilyn / Frogkisser / Neptunia / DizzieLizzie / OneElleofagirl / ShrinkingViolet / BengalLike- TheTiger / Betterin3D / Babygurl / TinyDancer / Sunny_side / Happy_Pepper / Smiley_spice / GoneFishing / Red_Nail_Polish / CultureVulture / CarpeDiem / HoorayForHedonism / IamMe / LastRolo? / LabradorOwner.*

Then, slightly smaller, came the subheaders: *Do you like Bob Dylan too? / I love romping in my wellies. / I love my Vespa, cupcakes and HBO. / I like all things Scandinavian, and vitamin D. / Sunshine, tea, F. Scott Fitzgerald, '70s glass kitchenware. / Lo-fi songs are great. / Je danse, donce je suis. / What is it about France and all things French? / I love the changing seasons. / I love food. / I love all things quirky. / I really detest the smell of oranges. / I'd date me. / Not your typical Mexican gal. / Curious about Mars. / Is this what it's come to? / Write something here. / Insert subheader of your choice. / In need of subheader inspiration. / Trying to think of something smart. / Do I have to do a subheader? / ??? / Well, this is embarrassing. / I work in finance *shudder*. / I'm a divorce lawyer in the city. / I'm looking for someone who is professional. / Woof. / I'm into beards. / Call off the dogs. / You're the one for me fatty. / Don't assume. / There's no lie in her fire. / I have magnificent breasts and an adequate personality. / Mostly after your money rofl. / I'm not very good at skiing. / Who cares if the glass is half full or half empty—fill* *it up! / A lot of people think I look like a vegetarian lesbian, but I love meat, as much as I can fit in my mouth at one time, and more. / I want to knit you a sweater, write you a love letter. / I milked a buffalo once. / Mucho gusto. / Proceed to checkout. / I am a contradiction. / Unconventional, kind, creative. / Unconventional, witty, kind. / Unconventional, creative, down-to-earth. / I wish I had a bigger garden.*

I snapped the laptop shut. I lay back and closed my eyes. I felt for the piece of cashmere under my pillow.

I could make myself appear on there too, couldn't I? I could try to work out a formula, an average of the profiles that had preceded me. I could find the median angle of the head tilt, and the mid-point cultural reference, and be part of that dizzying sequence of repetitions.

I had better take a look at the men, then, I supposed. I sat back up and I scrolled past pictures of writers and lawyers, environmentalists and bankers, young professionals, itinerants, filmmakers and clean-freaks. And then I saw something that really caught my eye: it was profile but the picture wasn't a man's head. Instead, it featured a geometric pattern—a matrix of cubes, subdivided into smaller and smaller triangles, spiraling into a disappearing centre. When I stared at the pattern, it created a 3-D tunnel effect: you could fall right into the picture. It was like a beautiful mineshaft. *I want to curate you*, the header read. And then, *Artist seeks swooning beauty. Must be able to take direction. Travel to Bedford required.*

Eight

I walked the streets watching my own progress ghosted by the little cipher on the screen of my phone. I had arrived at the train station and now I moved away from the centre of the town, along suburban roads. The evening was warm, but there was a soft drizzle beginning to fuzz the air. When I reached the place where the house was meant to be, a long driveway led away off the road. I turned along it, following until it bent sharply to the left into the grounds of a large house. The house looked as though it had once been a handsome family home—it had a red-tiled roof and 1920s proportions. The garden was enormous. I turned around in it. There was a large square lawn and borders full of buddleia. In the centre of the lawn was a wooden structure: a horse made out of something like willow. The garden had a freshly deserted feel to it, as though children had just been spooked into running away, and their voices might trail back on the wind at any moment.

I pushed the buzzer for flat 4 and the front door of the house vibrated with a release mechanism. There was a lot of post in the hallway, which had been swept to one side. Flat 1 was straight ahead of me, and a staircase led up to the first floor. I heard a door open somewhere above me, so I took the stairs. In one of the doorways stood a short, lean man, with mascara-black hair. He had a coiffed moustache and a severe strip of beard scoring vertically down the centre of his chin. He held out his hand to me.

Esther? he said, looking me up and down, giving nothing away. I'm Sam. Come on in.

I followed him into the flat. He was barefoot on bare floorboards. There would be none of the usual first-date small-talk, I could tell already. We turned into a large room with a fireplace. There was hardly any furniture in here; around the room various objects were staged as though they were exhibits. There was a chest next to the door, on top of which was arranged: a string of rosary beads, a pack of cards, a voodoo doll, a plastic leprechaun. An animal skull, a cow's perhaps, was positioned on the mantelpiece, and large flowers had been fixed in the empty eye-sockets. In the far corner of the room there was a large glass display case, filled with dead beetles.

These are some of my pieces, Sam said. You might have seen another in the garden.

Oh, right, I said. The horse?

I'm thinking of burning it down, he said. Perhaps tonight?

Oh, I said. Right. Sure. That sounds... fun.

Can I get you a drink? Perhaps some weed tea?

Weed tea?

Yes, he said, slowing his voice as if he might be dealing with an idiot. Weed, brewed into a tea.

Oh, right. Yeah. Lovely. Thank you.

He turned out of the room gracefully and returned shortly after with two teacups. Fuzzy bits of green floated at the top of the water.

The Lost Art of Sinking

We can sit together on the floor, he said. And get to know one another.

I sipped the tea, little fronds of green catching between my teeth. I chewed on them, then swallowed.

It's a much quicker way to get high, he said, and laughed. So, have you ever worked with an artist before?

No, not exactly, I said.

I could feel a softness beginning to loosen my tongue and I found that I wanted to talk and talk.

Maybe I'll be a natural? I said. You never know. My mother was a dancer, and very beautiful. She posed for some portraits. We have some photos of her dancing, bending all the way back and closing her eyes. And her grandmother was a music-hall performer. We have some early photos of her that look like paintings. They've touched up the colours, I think. It's so unnatural, so vivid.

I was talking quickly. I was definitely getting high.

Sam was stroking his moustache.

He laughed. I think we can make something beautiful together, he said. There's something in those eyes.

He stared at my face, and then down at my body.

How are you enjoying your tea?

The tea was making me feel... bizarre. I was switching rapidly between the desire to talk, and the desire to be inert.

Sam began to tell me about himself. He told me that the house we were in was empty. The landlord was selling to developers and all the other tenants had left. But he was refusing to go. He'd been holding exhibitions and parties in the garden all summer long.

I wanted to be on the floor. I lay down and let my weight sink into the floorboards.

But small, inanimate things seemed to tick into life at the edges my vision: the flower petals of the chrysanthemums seemed to crinkle spontaneously; the legs of the dead beetles seemed to flinch.

Sam was still talking.

I like burning things, he said at some point, though I'd lost track of what he was saying.

I was beginning to think I should be afraid of him, though I couldn't make myself feel alarmed. My body felt too soupy for that.

I kept my eyes on him. He was playing with a lighter, thumbing it to produce a flame.

Ow, he said, catching himself on the hot metal. And then he leant over towards me.

Can I kiss you, Esther? he asked, suddenly sounding earnest.

I was unsure. I began to try to say, *Maybe later...* but my lips barely moved.

I had never been this stoned. I was so high I was struck dumb.

Sam was attractive. His body was tight-knit with energy. As he leant over, I let him kiss me. He was forceful and his tongue moved rapidly.

Objects were still flickering at the edges of my vision. I felt a sharp sting against my arm. I pulled away—I *could* still move then. Thank fuck. I drew my arm back. There was a small red mark on it, in the shape of a horseshoe.

It didn't hurt so much at first, but then, as I looked at it, it started to bite into my flesh.

Sam was holding the lighter in his right hand.

It hurts, doesn't it? he said, excitedly. I wanted you to feel it too.

The Lost Art of Sinking

Then he got up and lifted a camera from the windowsill.

Now, this is what I'd like you to do, he said. I'm working on a series of pictures, as you know. The idea is, I'll restrict your oxygen intake, until you're just at the edge of unconsciousness. It's a wonderful feeling. It's euphoric. And it's perfectly safe. I've done this lots of times. Here—have a look at these pictures while I get my lighting kit.

He handed over the camera. Miniatures were displayed in the screen on the back. The first few images were of Sam himself—laid out, naked, in front of the fireplace, where I was lying now. There was a fire in the grate behind him and a belt around his neck. In the first couple of pictures his face was puce and his body taut, straining against auto-asphyxiation. In the final picture his body was relaxed, eyes closed, his head angled backwards. After this, there were pictures of girls lying naked in exactly the same position. Some of them had the belt around their necks. Some of them didn't. He'd taken close-ups of some of their faces, just before they passed out, their eyes glittering desperately.

I thought I could hear a scrabbling sound, as though beetles were skittering across the wooden floor.

I thought of the empty house and the empty garden, dark now, around us.

I became aware of a cloying, sweet smell in the flat, like decomposing organic matter.

When Sam came back into the room, he was carrying a belt.

We can do this any way you'd like, he said. I can use the belt, or I can do it manually and just restrict your air-flow with my hands.

He squatted down beside me. And when he leant in to kiss me again, my right hand swung up into his face in a fist, smacking him hard on the side of the jaw. It knocked him backwards.

I was as surprised as he was.

He clutched his face.

What the fuck? he shouted. Why did you do that? What's wrong with you?

I sat up, with some effort, and shook my head.

Shit, sorry, I said. Really. I didn't mean to. Let's just try again? You don't need to use the belt. I can put myself under, just give me a second.

He got up onto his feet, rubbing at his jaw.

If you weren't comfortable, you could just have said. This is why I went through everything beforehand, in the messages, he said. To make sure you were okay with everything.

I know, I said. I think it's the tea. Paranoia or something. I thought the beetles were moving.

I looked over at the glass case.

Sleep it off, he said. You can stay here, and then go in the morning.

Can't we try again? I asked.

Sam shook his head.

I'm not coming near you, he said.

Nine

It was still raining. It had been raining all summer long. People drove the revolving doors of the newspaper building open, clutching newspapers over their heads, their suits drenched a darker shade of grey around their makeshift rain-shelters.

One especially damp and dull day, I decided to walk up to Hampstead Heath after work. It was a short uphill burst in the drizzle—past large art-deco blocks of flats and then past enormous, gated white houses. When I reached the narrow streets at the centre of Hampstead Village, I wandered around them, looking for a coffee shop that might be Thomas's. There are beautiful old Georgian houses that have been converted into shops up here. Copper kitchenware was laid out in one brightly lit window. In another, there were mannequins draped in loose, bright clothes. There were windows full of glowing blue bottles, filled with organic beauty potions. The smell of mandarin blossom trailed me down the street.

I crossed the main road to take a narrow set of stone steps, which wound upwards between terraced houses, leading into a ginnel. It was almost like a village in the Pennines up here. At the very top, there was a break in the buildings and I could suddenly see all the way across London: the knobbled BT Tower was in the foreground; and then, softly fuzzed in the peach sky behind it, was the wheel. Other buildings that I didn't recognise were in the distance, where the orange-pink sky blurred into grey, like the flesh of cooked salmon darkening at the edges. I carried on walking. Small pubs were hidden away up here, already full of gregarious after-work drinkers. Finally, in a narrow passageway, I peered into a coffee-shop window. The sign on the door said *Closed*.

There was a man at the counter, with his back turned to the window. A tea-towel was wrapped around one of his hands. He was disengaging nozzles from a coffee machine and then rinsing them in the sink. After a few moments he turned around: it was Thomas. At that moment a woman, who had been sitting, unnoticed by me, at one of the tables, stood up and moved to meet him. They embraced. Thomas's hands were in the woman's hair. Watching this felt fucking thrilling. I was mesmerised by them getting into each other like that. I was ghosting the woman, standing in the same position as her. When they disentangled, I moved back from the window. I flattened myself against the wall. I waited a few moments, my heart beating hard. Then the woman banged the coffee-shop door open and walked away.

My legs moved me rapidly after her, across the street and back down the hill. There was real momentum in my body. The two of us were moving in series back down the high street towards Swiss Cottage. The woman walked very quickly. When we got down to Avenue Road, the woman made a sharp right, and my feet followed. She diverted into the big concrete box of the leisure centre, and I found myself behind her at the barriers. Then I was watching her back disappearing through another set of doors.

I'm sorry, said the woman on the front desk. Suzi's class is fully booked this evening.

Suzi's class? I turned to face the woman.

Yes, Suzi's hot yoga, the woman tilted her head towards where the woman had disappeared. I can book you in for her class tomorrow evening though, if you want? she said.

Oh, yes please, I said.

The heat hit me like a solid force when I entered the room. And then there was the smell. People were already sweating freely. One man, standing on his mat in just speedos, was supple with sweat. I picked a spot towards the back of the room. I rolled out the mat I'd borrowed from the centre. I lay down on it and breathed deeply. The lights were dim. Suzi entered the room, picking her way through the group to the front. She held herself beautifully, chin tilted slightly upwards, limbs fully articulated, as though her whole body was perfectly choreographed from her navel.

She moved like a dancer.

She moved like my mother had, and I thought for a moment that I might be about to cry or scream or run towards her or something.

The mat is bread, your body is butter, Suzi said in an affected voice. Melt your body into the mat.

After a cycle of nostril breathing, where I had to try hard not to succumb to the temptation to pass out, Suzi talked the class through sun salutations.

Listen to my instructions, she said. She was working hard to keep her voice soft, but she sounded annoyed. Don't look at the people around you. They're probably doing it wrong.

I followed her directions and moved my body through a sequence of bends and lunges and genuflections. The heat was really something.

If you're new to hot yoga, lie down if you need to, Suzi said. The body needs to adjust to the heat. But you. Must. Not. Leave. The room. Sudden temperature drop is *extremely* detrimental.

Suzie patrolled the rows as she barked out the next position: downward dog. I pushed my weight backwards, lifting my bum into the air. Suzi approached down the line, and when she reached me she put her hands on the base of my back, pushing me further backwards.

The pressure Suzi exerted against my body was firm and disinterested.

Spread your hands flat, Suzi said, they should be flat against the floor.

She pushed me a little harder, so that my face moved closer to the mat, and then she moved off to adjust someone else.

I was light-headed. If I looked to the right, I could see all of us in the mirrored wall in parallel.

When I rose up to standing, my vision began to swim.

The heat pushed itself more fiercely around and into my body. It was almost too much to bear. I began to move towards a backbend.

Do *not* close your eyes. Suzi was right in front of me. You'll lose balance. *Awareness* in the room please.

I had to open my eyes. In fact, I suddenly felt fantastically clear headed, as though my consciousness was beating against the heat.

Suzi continued with her firm instructions as she paced down the rows. As the postures got more advanced, she commanded the class with more obvious annoyance.

She talked us through a headstand: If you do not follow my instructions exactly, you will INJURE YOUR NECK, she shouted. Everyone can do this, if you just follow my instructions, she said. I don't understand why *some people* can't just follow instructions.

And then she reeled around and pointed at a woman on the front row.

Except you. You can't do this. Lie on your back.

As Suzi ordered us all to melt into our mats, the angry little catch in her voice kept drawing me back into consciousness.

The evening was still light when I emerged from the sports centre. I had showered, scrubbing at my face with hand soap. I felt super clean and exposed. I took the tube to Waterloo. And then I walked towards the river, intending to walk home as far as I could along its banks. On the South Bank were flamenco dancers and children screaming on a giant trampoline. The sun was just about to sink below the buildings on the opposite bank—blindingly bright in its final moments. My skin felt raw. I imagined it accumulating all of the dirt and pollution in the air. I kept on walking. I passed the Houses of Parliament. I passed grand cast-iron lampposts decorated with huge fish, which seemed to regurgitate the lamps themselves and the city around us like in the manner of a magic trick. As the towers of Battersea Power Station appeared on the horizon, the streetlights became fluorescent strips, and the other people thinned out. I approached a man who was sat on a bench, talking animatedly. There didn't seem to be anybody material he was talking to; I thought he must be on hands-free. The man was wearing a green anorak and, as I drew alongside him, I could see a polyester skirt and a blouse and pair of shoes laid out next to him on the bench. He had dressed the empty silhouette of a woman. He continued to speak to the clothes as I passed him by.

I carried on walking until the path at the side of the Thames disappeared into riverside apartments and the sky had become grey. Then I was forced into Vauxhall and I drifted until I found the tube.

Later, deep in the night, I woke. I lay in the dark and thought of Veronica asleep in the room below me; and then of the hundreds of people hidden in sleep along our street, and on all the other streets of Colliers Wood, so many sleeping people whom I would never know, and who would never know me. I lay there in the dark, a secret to them, to all the unmourning strangers of London.

We were all composed of the same stuff, weren't we? Organic tissue and bone. Dark matter. But I had so little experience of the body's interior. I thought of Jay in that little box room in the Cherry Street house. Exsanguinated. The sight of blood. That had a transporting effect on people, didn't it? The sight of blood. Perhaps I should go to the hospital? Perhaps I should do what Veronica wanted of me?

I clicked back my skylight blind to let some starlight in. I watched the winking planes circle, low and wide over the city, like a night-time vigil over all our dark bodies.

My breathing slowed and I was folded back into sleep.

Ten

St George's Hospital was sheened linoleum and speed-walkers as far as the eye could see. Which was not very far: vision was limited by the low-ceilinged corridors and their sharp corners. I followed the signs for Phlebotomy, which took me out of the main building, across two car parks, and then back into a squat '60s prefab.

I introduced myself at the desk.

Oh, right, the work experience girl? said a tired-looking woman in a thin blue pyjamas.

Well, I said. I—my cousin, Veronica, works here, and she—

The woman wasn't listening to me. She'd already picked up the phone and put a call through.

Freestone here for you, she said.

A few moments later a young, gorgeously fat woman bustled into the waiting room in green overalls.

You must be Esther, she said, without breaking her walk. She signalled for me to follow her.

I'm Carmilla, she said as we quick-stepped down a corridor. I've heard such a lot about you from Vron. She's so pleased you're coming in.

I followed Carmilla into an examination room. She motioned for me to take a seat.

So... Carmilla wound a strand of blond hair behind her ear and scanned a clipboard.

We'll be seeing lots of different people today for lots of different blood tests. You'll get a good sense of the range of patients that we deal with here. It's varied work, though there's always a needle involved. Ha!

Carmilla's voice was soft and refined and sexy; she was slightly breathless.

Some of them are regulars here, she said. Others might never have had a blood test before. She checked her watch. We've got a few minutes, so I can go over the equipment with you.

Carmilla got out several small drawers full of plastic-wrapped apparatus.

Okay, this is what we use most commonly, she said, for a straightforward venopuncture, where we want to draw blood from here.

She turned her own arm tender side up, rolled up the long-sleeved top she was wearing under her overalls.

So, you can't see much at the moment, she said, but the cubital fossa, anterior to the elbow, is the best place to draw blood. The median cubital vein is close to the surface and has minimal nerve supply.

I watched Carmilla continue to massage her flesh: at first I could only see the tiny dark-blue threads close to the surface of her skin, so delicate they looked like biro lines. But then a vein began to rise in a small greenish bulge.

So, on this kind of vein we'd usually go for a vacuum tube, she said. Don't worry, you don't need to remember all this!

Carmilla rolled her sleeve back down and shook one of the plastic packets.

The Lost Art of Sinking

You'll see a lot of these today, she said. We only use one hypodermic needle, and multiple vacuum tubes can be attached if we need to take multiple samples from the patient.

Carmilla tossed the packet back in a drawer.

You can use a fingerstick for small tests. Or, if you are dealing with a very small baby, a neonatal heelstick. Do you want tea and a biscuit? You look a little bit pale, my darling.

Carmilla placed her hand on my arm and gave it a firm squeeze.

You're not squeamish are you, you lovely thing? We haven't even seen any blood yet! I'm going to get you a cup of tea and a biscuit.

When she moved, her overalls rustled like paper.

I stared at the lucent floor tiling; it had been polished until the plastic looked like solid liquid.

It was unsettling to see Carmilla's vein beneath the surface of her skin—that little glut of blue-green, a tiny glimpse of the territory underneath; inside. I felt a dizzying swirl in my stomach at the thought of the blood to come.

Carmilla came back with two plastic cups of tea, biscuits stacked up high on top of each one. She cooed over me for a while, making me drink the sugary tea, and then she talked me through the different tubes that are used in different blood tests: some came ready-prepared with additives to prevent the blood from clotting; others, for tests in which clotting time is at stake, contained citrates; some were laced with clotting accelerators. It would be my job today to hand over the correct tubes, under Carmilla's instruction.

The first patient was a regular, Carmilla explained: a heavily pregnant woman who was rhesus negative. She was being tested regularly because her baby was at risk of erythroblastosis fetalis: To put it simply, Carmilla said, the mother's antibodies might travel through the placenta and attack the red blood cells in fetal circulation, the blood cells the baby needed.

The mother and baby's blood is a shared system, Carmilla said, but sometimes it turns *nasty*.

Carmilla buzzed through to reception, and, a few moments later, a pregnant woman pushed her way in and sat down heavily.

How are you today, Ruth? Carmilla asked.

Tired, said the woman. Work are breathing down my neck about coming in late after all these tests.

Right, well let's get on with it then. Left today.

Carmilla pulled on latex gloves and directed me towards the correct tube. Then she fixed it to the gleaming hypodermic. The woman had already pulled up her sleeve and was looking away, disinterested, towards the door. Carmilla palpated the stretched crux of the woman's arm, gently, tenderly, as she had her own—and sure enough, a bluer vein began to rise up. She positioned the needle and eased it gently into the skin, so that the moment of incision was impossible to detect. And then the tube began to fill.

The colour of the blood in the light blue room was incredible; it bloomed upwards, a lurid and gorgeous coagulation.

I was drawn towards it. I couldn't help it. I started to hyperventilate, so subtly that they couldn't have heard me.

The woman's face flickered as the needle retracted. But otherwise, once Carmilla had whipped the tube away, it was almost inconceivable that the woman was made of blood: that, underneath her floral maxi-dress and mesh of skin, an intricate bloodwork was progressing inside her; that between the matted blood placenta and the gathering blood of the new baby, there was a complex and potentially treacherous blood ecology.

I remembered the word *exsanguinated*, and felt my pulse tick in my lips and my cheeks. I let my head fall backwards a little and closed my eyes.

Esther, are you okay? Carmilla clamped a hand on her shoulder.

Oh, I'm fine, I said, and brought my head upright.

Carmilla was too vigilant; I'd never get away with anything.

Not all the patients were as straightforward to bleed as the first. There was an elderly woman later in the morning whose veins looked as though they were tougher than any other patient's: they rose up through the skin of her arms, fat and solidly blue, as soon as she clenched her fist. But apparently her veins were collapsing. She was a regular too. Carmilla asked me to find her a butterfly needle, and she tried a new approach, through a tiny new vein that Carmilla thought might be branching off the collapsing course. The woman's arm was so thin that there was nothing plump to rest the point of the needle against; the insertion looked more like a blind stab. And it didn't work the first time. The blood clotted too quickly and stopped being drawn up the tube. The old woman leaned her head back and groaned. Her arm was covered in old bruises.

I looked for these new branching veins, the new tributaries splitting off where the old had failed. I remembered something from Biology: that blood vessels are fractal, branching under the skin again and again and again.

Finally, Carmilla extracted a sample she could use—and the woman hugged herself, as though protecting herself from further violence.

Our final patient of the morning blundered into the room and came to a halt right in front of us. His gait was strange: he held himself tall, chest barrelled, as though squaring up for a fight, but his arms hung limp from his torso. I realised he must be drunk, because of the smell. And then I saw that he was already bleeding: there was blood spattered down his bare right leg, blackening on the fabric of his shorts. This was no longer as odd as it would have been a few hours ago. The blood was merely in the wrong place. I followed the line of splatter upwards and saw that the end of the man's middle finger was a raggedy glut of blood.

Mr Stevens? Jack, isn't it?

Carmilla was up on her feet, deftly steering the man into a chair.

You're bleeding already, my darling. I'm just going to call someone to see to that. She picked up her phone and requested an auxiliary to dress a wound.

Now then, Jack, you need to tell us what happened to your finger.

The man extended his legs out, rigid.

Can't remember, can I? he said. Woke up in the shed. And then I was rushing to get here. Late. Must've caught it on something.

He had left a smudge of blood across his forehead, and now his finger was dripping onto the linoleum. A knock at the door, and a woman with a plastic case came in. She smiled kindly at the man, and he held his hand out like a child towards her. The woman cleaned it and dressed it, and then it looked like an enormous white bulb.

Ha! said the man.

Another woman came into the room to clean and disinfect the floor.

Can nurse get you something for the pain? Carmilla asked.

Can't feel a thing, the man responded.

Carmilla took blood from his other arm. He didn't seem to notice.

You need to take better care of yourself, Jack, she said.

No one to care if I take care of myself or not, he said, cheerfully.

The results will come through to your doctor, Carmilla said, and showed him out. And then she turned back to me.

Now then, you've got the blood in your cheeks back, young lady, she said.

Veronica met me outside the entrance to A&E. She was wearing green pyjamas and her hair was pulled back into a ponytail.

So, how was it? she asked as we walked together through the car park. You didn't freak out, did you?

No, not exactly, I said. I thought it was pretty... amazing actually.

It was drizzling again: a gauze over the road in front of us.

Right? said Veronica. Okay? So shall we look into phlebotomy training for you?

Oh, I said. No. I mean, I wouldn't be any good for the patients.

Veronica turned her face skywards and raised her palms in a gesture of *give-me-strength*.

I don't understand you, Ettie, she said. What is it that you want to *do* with your life?

Veronica's phone rang from behind her. She shrugged off her rucksack and dug out her phone.

Hello? She listened for a moment and then passed the phone across to me. It's your father, she said. He's being dramatic.

Eleven

It rained all the way up to Leeds. As the train pulled out of King's Cross, a woman with bright yellow hair pushed a trolley down the aisle, calling out sandwiches and coffee in a market cadence.

It rained all the way across to Todmorden.

Blue and brown fields streaming past.

We have a rainy season now, one old man on the train was saying to another. I couldn't see their faces, but their words came in long, low rumbles, with great pauses in between.

Just. Like. India.

The water on the window was collecting in multiplying beads, which must, I thought, be convulsing as they travelled at speed, clinging to the train. But the convulsion was imperceptible. The beads seemed entirely still, until they suddenly streamed away.

It's global. Warming. Isn't. It?

Field upon field of cabbages blurred past. Glimmering blue lakes of greens.

Then why. Aren't. We any. Warmer. Eh?

As we pulled into the valley, I could see that the fields either side of the canal, which should be green, were covered in still brown water.

The whole valley bottom was brown.

Doesn't. Work. Like. That. It's. The Gulf. Stream. Being affected.

What was strange was the stillness of the water. It was as though it had always been there, as though the playing fields had never existed. The green had disappeared so absolutely.

I *don't*. Know.

My father picked me up from the train station in his 4x4. When we got to the bottom road, where the street crosses the river, brown surface water covered the tarmac and all of the gutters were gushing. Cars drove slowly, kicking up water around them.

This is much better! my father said. Yesterday it was practically impassable. And further down it was completely flooded. Waist deep. We were cut off for a couple of days. We've had reports of cars stranded and people wading to safety up at Morrisons. All sorts of things. We're running a story on an elderly woman living between the canal and the river. The water flooded her house a couple of nights ago, and she was trapped upstairs with her miniature poodle for twelve hours. Nobody could get near her. Five feet of it, pouring from the river into the canal through her house. She spent most of the night talking on the phone to my reporter.

We turned off the main road and drove over the bridge to the house. There was very little surface water left here, but there was a residual brown soddenness.

The garden looked as though it had leaked slurry: filthy wetness swelling up out of the ground.

Inside the house, the smell was terrible: salty, sludgey, ancient sourness.

The Lost Art of Sinking

There was an oily film of water covering the carpets.

Look what the council helpfully dropped off, my dad said.

He motioned towards a box on the kitchen table.

Tins of spam and sandbags!

I took my things upstairs. The bedrooms hadn't gotten wet, but the electricity was off, so everything felt even more dismal than usual. I changed my clothes and quickly checked on her studio. It was the same: unalterably green and gloomy.

I spent the next few hours helping Dad to sort through his effects, separating the recoverable from the terminally sodden. Then we started to move things upstairs or outside, so that he could take up the wet carpets and set things out to dry. There was an anxious whirring in the background: the sound of the pump pulsing water out of the cellar. I surprised a frog in the sideboard and there were small black leeches clinging to the skirting boards.

I was down on my hands and knees, forcing more water up out of carpet, when I found it. I was sorting through the things in the bottom of the dresser. There were boxes full of records in here, which might have been recoverable. And then I came across an old tin, embossed in gold, with an art-nouveau woman iconised on the lid. The tin seemed to spring open in my hands and it was full of small, beautiful things. A ring, a glittering brooch, a little cut-glass cube. I picked the cube up. It was familiar. It looked like a squat salt shaker, full of white powder. But instead of perforations on the top, there was a battered silver screw cap.

It had lived on her drink's cabinet, that's where I recognised it from. It was one of Moira's curiosities.

Dad walked back into the room. He froze on the threshold when he saw what was in my hands.

Put that box down, please, Esther, he said. His voice had gone all formal.

What is this? I said, turning the cube up to the light. I always wanted to know, but I never asked... her.

It's... it's something your mother inherited. From her grandmother, he said.

He stepped towards me.

Smelling salts. Salt of hartshorn, I think. Made from ground up hart's antlers, supposedly. It'd burn out your mucus membranes if you weren't careful.

He was being horribly jovial with his voice now.

It supposedly stopped you from fainting. And your great-grandmother was a fine one for pretending she was always about to faint. An actress, as you know.

He placed a hand on my shoulder.

Let's put these old things away, he said, reaching out towards the tin.

It was then that I spotted it: slantways between the glittering glass and dull metal. A violet envelope. I snatched it out of the tin.

The word *Esther* curled across the front in my mother's writing.

My father let his hand fall away from me.

Please, he said. Please. Just put it all away.

He staggered backwards.

I can't, he said, I can't look at these things now.

I watched him, crumpled and pink-cheeked, sliding slowly down the wall.

I hadn't seen her writing in so long. I couldn't just put it away again.

The envelope's tongue was folded tightly into its mouth

and the paper rasped as I opened it. Inside the envelope was a note, and more of my mother's elaborate handwriting.

Dear Esther, I'm sorry. I'm sorry that I have to leave you. I wish you'd had a better mother. I love you. I hope you can feel that—despite everything. Moira.

And that was it. The words ended there. No affectionate sign-off, no little kisses.

I stared across at my father. I read over the paragraph again.

What is this? I asked.

My father was still slumped against the wall.

Your mother was very ill, at the end, he said. Paranoid. Most of all drunk.

So she wrote this just before she died? She knew she was about to die?

He looked at me with a strange expression then. With a question in his face.

Yes, Esther, she knew.

I looked at the letter again, but I couldn't keep the words still.

I was shivering.

So, she was at peace with... leaving us? I asked.

Not at peace, for god's sake, Esther. Not at all at peace. She refused treatment, and then she... *did* it.

It?

She had looked so beautiful when I found her. When I arrived home from school and called up to her and there had been no reply. When I walked the dark staircase and called again. When I raised the alarm, crying on the phone to the emergency services like a baby gull, crying on the phone to my father. Those long, long minutes when I was alone with her. The green light of the canal spilling through her room. Spilling across her cold skin.

Then people were ushering me out of her room and they'd taken her away.

But when I found her—her body finalised like that, leaning backwards over her chaise—she had looked totally serene.

She choreographed the whole thing, my father is saying. I'm sorry to say it, Esther, but she must have known you would find her. I didn't know how... I didn't know when to tell you.

He slid down to the floor and pressed his thumbs into his eyelids.

I walked out of the house. I walked over the bridge and into town. The water was flowing in the usually-still canal and it looked close to flooding again. I walked onto the main road. I walked past the Aldi, where a woman in green overalls was sweeping water out of the front door. I kept along the main road. All of the shops were closed, and people inside were sweeping their floors of water and silt. There were mounds of sodden carpet blocking the pavement. The sour green sludge smell followed me everywhere.

The graveyard wasn't flooded, though the ground was turned to bog in places. The parkland next to the church is part of the flood-defence system, so the river had been diverted there. It was now one enormous brown pool, with a red climbing frame rising from its centre.

I walked between the graves. Leanne's house stood up ahead, interposing itself between the A646 and the dead.

The Lost Art of Sinking

There were some boys over in the corner of the grave-yard that is nearest the woods—three of them, wearing their anoraks zipped right up and smoking reefers. I could smell the greenness of the skunk they were smoking through the damp air.

I kept going until I found her grave. There were tiny gold-finches darting around in the trees above it, like fluttering leaves. I lay down on the sodden ground to watch them. I could feel the water soaking into my hair and around the skin on my skull. I could hear the boys laughing, and I thought of the skunk burning orange in their fingers, and then moving with their breath into their lungs. I pictured their bronchioles, the tiny vessels splitting again and again, the hot smoke moving through these pathways. And then I looked at the woods behind them. At the patch of trees that had survived centuries of deforestation on the valley side, their branches forking into the grey sky. And beneath the trees, deep in the soil, I knew there would be a network of mycelia keeping the wood alive, fine filaments travelling downwards from the fruiting bodies of the fungi—from the Liberty Caps and super-strong Fly Agaric—down through the black earth, spreading tree-like underground and nourishing the wood above with oxygen and occult information.

When I closed my eyes, I could see the branching pattern still. I couldn't tell if it was an imprint of the branches in the sky, or an image of mycelium, or an X-ray vision of a lung, or the veins of my own eyelids flashing before me.

I listened to the water. If I concentrated hard, I could hear the water gurgling, even above the sound of the boys' voices. I could hear it travelling all the way from the moortops, soaking through the ancient millstone grit at the very top of the valley, washing down the Flower Scar road, running off the sandstone on the tops, running through the heather and into the coal seams, into the soft mudstone beneath, gushing through valley sides, gushing right down here into the valley bottom and flooding the streets and sewers.

If I lay here long enough, perhaps I would begin to break down. Perhaps I'd be reconstituted as the sodden ground of the valley. My skin, the thick pad of it, bloating into earth.

My body was beginning to do it. Force of habit. My breathing was speeding up, ready to shut down.

Maybe I'd be out long enough for the water to dissolve me?

But here's the thing: I couldn't do it. I couldn't pass out.

My breathing accelerated.

And nothing happened.

I gasped the air harder. I held it in.

And here I still was.

Cold and totally conscious.

Are you unwell? a woman's voice asked above me. Are you able to stand?

I opened my eyes.

An elderly woman wearing a rain hat was standing over me.

Oh, I said. Sorry. Yes, I can stand. Don't worry. I was just—

Well then get onto your feet, young lady, the woman said. Frightening me like that. Don't you know we're in the middle of a flood?

The woman walked briskly away down the path and then turned back to check on me.

I got up onto my feet. The obverse of my body was cold and wet.

The Lost Art of Sinking

The woman was kneeling on a cushion in front of a flower bed now, and she drew a trowel from a basket.

Well, are you helping or are you hindering? she asked.

I walked towards her.

I'll help you, I said. If I can.

Now then, she said. These plants are waterlogged. We need to make a course around the roots of each plant, so that the water can drain, and then we're going to add some sand to the soil.

The woman turned to glare at me again.

You can do the sand, she said. I planted all of these, you know, the woman said. A group of us do it. Wherever there's unused land, we've planted it. We've done legumes in front of the police station, and fruit trees in the supermarket borders, and herbs around the health centre. Now I'm cultivating from the dead. Ha!

She hummed a little tune, and then she turned on me again with her goitrous blue eyes.

And why are you falling down in graveyards, young lady?

I stared at the ground. I had no idea what to say.

Are you on drugs? she asked.

I laughed then.

No, I said.

The woman continued to scoop away at the earth and said nothing for a while. Then: Do you know, we share thirty-five per cent of our genetic coding with daffodils? Did you know that? the woman said. Remarkable isn't it?

I thought of the daffodils that my father has planted above my mother's grave, which have sprung up each year since her death, nosing their way through the earth. Repeating themselves. Flinching brightly in the breeze.

Naomi Booth

The woman turned her attention back to the raspberry bushes.

I leaned over her and poured the sand in circles round the roots of the plant.

When I stood up again, I felt something bloom through my abdomen. A gorgeous arterial gush.

I looked up to the horizon. I was right back at the start of all of this. Wisp of a moon in the watery sky. Dusk descending over the hills, a line of light illuminating the moortops. A dog was crying somewhere. Sound travels strangely in the valley: the animal might have been close by, or miles above us on the sodden moors.

I hadn't passed out. I couldn't pass out. I had lost my art.

I followed the old woman around the graveyard.

Slowly, carefully, I shadowed the woman's movements in sand as the rain began, again, to fall.

Acknowledgements

I am forever grateful to Penned in the Margins and Tom Chivers for first publishing this work, and for allowing it to be re-published here. Thank you to all at Dead Ink, and to my indefatigable agent, Sabhbh Curran, for bringing this new edition to life. I wrote *The Lost Art of Sinking* while I was researching the literary history of swooning at Sussex University, and I am grateful to the Arts and Humanities Research Council for funding that research, and to Nicholas Royle for teaching me so much during it. I would like to thank the following people for their generous friendship, brilliant advice, and patient reading of early versions of this book: Camilla Bostock, Tom Bunstead, Michael Fake, Dulcie Few, Thomas Houlton, Kieran Devaney, Laura Joyce, Helen Jukes, Kate Murray-Browne, Toby Smart. Thank you, also, to those who supported the book when it was first published, including my mum and dad (who helped me in myriad practical ways, even though the book is, 'a bit weird'), Abi Curtis, Nasser Hussain, Sarah Jackson, Sophie Nicholls, the Saboteur Awards team, New Writing North and all of the brilliant libraries and librarians in the North of England who hosted me for Read Regional events.

About the Author

Naomi Booth is the author of *Sealed*, *Exit Management* and *Animals at Night*. She is the recipient of a Saboteur Award for Best Novella and was named a *Guardian* Fresh Voice in 2019. Her short fiction has been longlisted for the *Sunday Times* EFG Short Story Award, the Galley Beggars Short Story Prize and anthologised in *Best British Short Stories*. Her story 'Sour Hall' was adapted into an Audible Originals drama series. Naomi grew up in West Yorkshire and now lives in York.

**Other titles by
Naomi Booth**

Animals at Night

"The man two doors down pursues a secret hobby in the dead of night.
This is one of your first discoveries."

The night invites strange happenings, strange meetings, strange thoughts.
A mother feeding her baby hears sounds in the city around her. A grieving
widow encounters an injured jellyfish on a deserted beach. A young
woman can't shake the image of a dying hare she finds at the side of the
road. A dairy farmer hears the herd bellow with fear at night.

Collected here are stories that illuminate nocturnal meetings between
humans and other animals in the eagerly anticipated first collection of
short fiction from acclaimed author, Naomi Booth.

Exit Management

"At minus eighteen degrees, even the densest blood materials start to turn: the beginnings of a human heart will still into black ice."

Callum has been given an opportunity: József's house is the perfect place to live – plenty of room, a sought-after London location and filled with priceless works of art. All that József asks in return is for some company while he's ill and the promise that if it all gets too much, someone will be there to help him at the end.

It's fortunate then, when Callum meets Lauren who works in Human Resources and specialises in getting rid of people. József welcomes them both inside, and so begins a deadly spiral of violence. Pushed ever onwards by the poison of ambition, and haunted by loses from the past, these characters are drawn together in a catastrophe of endings.

Sealed

"We came out here to begin again. We came out here for the clear air and a fresh start. No one said to us: beware of fresh starts. No one said to us: God knows what will begin."

Heavily pregnant Alice and her partner Pete are done with the city. Above all, Alice is haunted by the rumours of the skin-sealing epidemic starting to infect the urban population. Surely their new remote mountain house will offer safety, a place to forget the nightmares and start their little family... but the mountains and their people hold a different kind of danger. With their relationship under intolerable pressure, violence erupts and Alice is faced with the unthinkable as she fights to protect her unborn child.

Timely and suspenseful, *Sealed* is a gripping modern fable on motherhood, a terrifying portrait of ordinary people under threat from their own bodies and from the world around them.

Animals at Night, Exit Management and *Sealed* are all available at

deadinkbooks.com